Mary

Give and Take

For my boys.
Thank you for being so good and letting Mommy write. Even when it was hard.
I LOVE ALL THREE OF YOU!

RUNNING AWAY WILL NEVER MAKE YOU FREE
-KENNY LOGGINS

THERE'S A FINE LINE BETWEEN RUNNING AND RUNNING AWAY
-CANNON BLACKWOOD

Prologue

NINE YEARS EARLIER

S o, what's the plan tonight?" I asked Jackie. Wait, no, what was her name? *Shit!* I had been staying at this chick's house for three months. I should remember her damn name. *It might be time to lay off the coke and weed.*

"Oh, I don't know, I think Marcus may come over and bring some blow," the girl answered in a cheery tone. Her voice was like nails on a proverbial chalkboard. *Coke? Again? Ugh. I'm not up for feeling spastic and then having the aftermath of the letdown.* She was three years older than me, I assumed. We really didn't do a whole lot of girl talk. *Shit, I can't even remember her damn — ah! Angel.*

She, like most people, was taller than me. Her hair was currently white and super short. It was shaved on the sides and back; the top, however was long enough to cover her brown eyes. We met where I tended to meet all of my friends — at a party. Oh, well, or through a drug dealer. When Angel saw I was between homes, she offered me her couch in exchange for me partying with her. Who was I to say no? Free place to stay for drugs and parties? Yeah, I think so.

"Hey, how about we call him? See if he has any white stuff?" I asked shyly. I would much rather party with some H than anything else. Snorting that gave me the high, but none of the come-down that came with blow.

"Oh, good idea! All of the high, none of the hangover," she replied, grabbing her phone.

I was trying not to shake at the thought of the high I knew would be coming. I glanced over at Angel. She murmured something unintelligible into the phone and then squeed like a fucking dolphin. My hands flew to my ears. For fuck's sake, she hit a pitch I thought might shatter glass. My eyes slid to the grime-covered window. Nope, still there.

"He's going to bring the stuff! And, he said to get ready for the high of your life!" Her white hair fell in her eyes and she blew it out of sight. She was smiling from ear to ear. My heart sped up. I had a hard time not smiling back at her.

This is my life. Bouncing from one home to the

next, looking to score my next high, hoping to God I didn't get arrested. The biggest and greatest thrill I would have was the thought — and the act — of getting high. Sixteen years old, school dropout, so damned damaged.

I shook my head in disgust and walked over to the window. I couldn't see a damn thing out of it due to the dirt that had been caked on. I ran a finger through it, inspecting the filth. It was the buildup from smoke. Smoke from crack, weed, heroin, and cigarettes. *I wonder, if I lick it, if I would get a little buzz.* What a singularly fucked-up thought. I wiped the grime on my pants.

I would ask how my life got so screwed up, but I knew just how it happened. My mom was a drunk and ruined her own life. I took her actions and ran with them, and now was just as big of a loser as she was. Maybe Aaron, my older brother, got out unscathed. Maybe he was on some island living the rich life. Maybe he had a family. Maybe he had replaced all thoughts of me. I would have.

My vision blurred with unshed tears. I tried to steel myself against my wild emotions. I hadn't cried since my time in the house of horrors. The one with the monstrous people who called themselves foster parents. And I didn't plan on starting now.

I ran the flat of my palm against the glass and wiped the dirt on my shirt. It was cold this time of year, but today was especially so. Atlanta never really got snow, other than the kind that never stuck to the ground. But, today, it was sticking. This house was tiny, with just a roof and couch, as we couldn't afford actual beds. I really couldn't complain.

The snow fell in sheets, but the flakes seemed to dance their way down to the ground. They hit the brown grass and stayed for a moment before another was added to the first. The sod was quickly coated in a thin blanket of the cold, white stuff. When I was little, I used to watch the snow like this. I used to look at it with wonder.

I recalled one night at my aunt and uncle's house. It had snowed just as it was tonight. One evening, after my uncle had his nightly visit, I ran out in the snow. We lived just north of Atlanta, far away from any big cities. The absence of light seemed to make the stars pop, and it made the snow seem whiter, somehow.

I remember running out into the frigid night, hoping that if I just ran fast enough, I could run to that place Dorothy talked about. If I ran hard enough, I could find that magical place hidden over the rainbow. I ran so fast that night. I dodged the falling flakes with ease. But, I never found the rainbow, much less the Emerald City. That was the night I gave up. The moment I stopped believing in a happy ending. But, it was also the night I knew I was different.

"Addison," Angel's shrill voice cut through the memories. I glanced back at her.

"What's up?" She had a weird expression on her face. She looked guilty.

Angel refused to meet my eyes when she said, "So, Marcus said this would be our last freebee."

My eyes widened at that. Neither of us had money. She was a stripper at a club downtown. But, she really didn't make enough to cover everything we smoked and snorted. Just how would we be expected to pay for drugs? Just goes to show how low I was, when it's not food or bills I worry about, it's drugs.

"So, what are we going to do?" She looked me up and down. Oh, hell no. I shook my head at her.

"Look, we need more money. If you still wanna get high, you need to get a job," she explained.

"I'm sixteen. What kind of job could I get?"

I crossed my arms over my small chest with the hope that she would stop eyeing me like I was a piece of meat.

"I have a buddy at the club. I can get you a job there."

"I'm sixteen. Isn't that illegal or something?" I asked.

She waved away my question as though it were a pesky gnat buzzing in her ear.

"I know what Marcus is bringing. You will want more. How about you answer me after? You tell me just what you would do for another hit."

I raised an eyebrow at her. Just what the hell was he bringing? Superman on a flying unicorn or some shit?

I returned my attention to the window. My life was such shit. I could run when I wasn't high. But I was high more often than I wasn't, so there was no running for me.

I had little time for brooding as I saw Marcus's car pull up to the sidewalk. He had a beat-up Camaro. It looked to be straight out of the '80s. But, at least he had a car. I couldn't judge. My heart began to pick up speed at the sight of his backpack. I knew what lay in that bag was some seriously good shit.

"Hey, Marcus is here," I called over my shoulder.

"Oh, hell yes!" Angel squealed as she raced to the front door that was just to my left. I took a few steps back to avoid the cool air, but it still brushed against my overheated skin. I breathed it in, hoping it would calm me.

"Sup, ladies." Marcus's smooth, low voice seemed to fill the room. The large, white man took up enough space for six men, despite the fact that he was only the size of two. He stood just south of six feet. He had stringy brown hair that hung to his shoulders. His body type was a lot like, well, a manatee. Round up top, and through the middle, and skinny legs. I often wondered how those toothpicks could hold up anything, much less his sloppy self. But, right now, he was fucking Fabio.

"Hey, Marcus."

He glanced over at me and took a long, lingering look from my head down to my chest, where he stayed for a prolonged moment, then to my feet. He smiled. I shivered at what I knew he was thinking. What every loser, druggy friend thought. I wanted to tell him to take his dick and shove it, but I really wanted the drugs, so I kept my mouth shut. Angel, however, had no issues sleeping with him. I shivered at the thought. *Yuck, so much yuck.*

"You girls ready to get this party started?" Marcus asked.

"Hell yes!" Angel replied, excitedly. She was practically vibrating.

I nodded, walked over to the couch and sat down.

"Hey, Angel, you got the works?" She nodded and ran toward the bathroom.

The works? What did that mean? Marcus took off his belt and set it down on the table. The buckle clattered down and I jumped at the sound.

"Relax, Addison. You're wound up," he remarked as he began pulling the contents of his backpack out on to the small, maple-colored table.

Just as I was about to question what he was doing, Angel ran back in the room with a small, wooden box. She plopped down next to me and opened the container.

Inside were about ten syringes and q-tips. My eyes widened. *Holy shit balls.* I had smoked H. I'd snorted it, too. But, I had never injected it. My heart rate kicked up another notch and my skin grew clammy. I couldn't do this, no fucking way.

Angel must have seen the panic in my eyes, because she placed a cool hand on my arm.

"Addison, I would never do something that would hurt you. You're like a sister to me." She gave my arm a light squeeze before removing her hand. I nodded.

I sat there just staring, transfixed by the actions of these two people as though they were in slow motion. Each twitch or jerking movement caused the steady beating of my heart to ratchet up to a more frantic pace. *God, Addison, what are you doing?* I saw Marcus pull out a spoon and couldn't watch this any longer. Without a word, I flew to the bathroom. I was beyond caring if they questioned my speed. Hell, even if they did confront me about being a pusher, I could blame it on the drugs.

The bathroom was more like a closet and it was in the same state as the rest of the house, filth covered. There was always a scent of old, dirty, mildew-covered towels. I gripped my hands on the counter and stared at my reflection in the mirror. My eyes were rimmed with deep, red circles that fanned out into purple bags. My face was thin. I knew I was underweight, but I hadn't really realized just how gaunt I was. My naturally wavy, blonde hair was stringy and fell in clumps, rather than its normal soft curls. My lips were slightly chapped. I could get past all of it, every bit of my physical appearance, except my eyes. They looked haunted and dead. I was slowly losing the fire that sparked behind them. I was turning into someone I barely recognized. *Will I still be a pusher if I do this?* I loved running as fast I did. I loved being able to move things with my mind, even if it was sporadic. Would I give it all up to get high? Did I care anymore?

I searched my eyes for the answers. The only thing I saw looking back at me were two blue orbs that had given up on nearly everything a long time ago. I turned the faucet on and splashed some much-needed water on my sweaty face. The cool liquid acted like an electrical shock to my system. I peered back up at myself. I looked the same as before, just wetter. I wasn't sure what I thought I would see or if I expected the water to fix me. But, it hadn't. I still looked haggard and broken. I sucked in a huge gulp of air and walked out of the bathroom.

Angel's eyes were glazed over and she was slightly slumped against the arm of the couch. I looked to Marcus, who motioned for me to sit down. I walked over and sat, trying to ready myself. My knees were shaking and my head was throbbing. My heart and my head were screaming that this was such a bad idea. But, I had heard about how good the high was from this shit. And that thought alone, honest to God, made my mouth water.

"You done it like this before?" I knew what he was asking. Had I ever shot up with dope before? I shook my head, not wanting to speak it out loud.

"Want me to do it for you?" Did I? Could I? Should I? Everything was screaming, "No, run away as fast as you possibly can." All but this tiny little voice screaming about just how amazing the high would feel. Just then, I heard moans coming from Angel's lips. They sounded sexual.

I nodded and he got up and moved around the small table. He pulled my arm to his lap, then slipped the thick brown belt up to the middle of my bicep and cinched it tight. The metal of the clasp bit into my skin, but my frantic heartbeat was so wild I hardly registered anything as pain.

"Wait."

It was a bare whisper of a sound, but he paused, his hand hovering above the needle that sat on the table.

He eyed me, not asking the question I knew he wanted to know the answer to.

"Will it hurt?" I asked. I wasn't sure why I asked this. Maybe I was stalling.

"Yeah, but it's like all things in life. Take a little pain for a lot of pleasure. It's give and take, Addison."

He moved to pick up the syringe, all while never taking his deep-brown eyes off mine. I tried desperately to swallow the lump in my throat, but it was impossible.

"You ready?" I looked down and the needle hovered only an inch from my skin. There would be no going back. I nodded.

The needle slid so effortlessly into my skin, it

seemed like it belonged there. He pulled back slightly and I saw blood flood the amber liquid. He reached up and took the belt off. Slowly, he injected it.

I sank back into the couch and closed my eyes. It all seemed to rush to my head. The world spun wildly out of control. My whole body felt light, like it was floating. This was a high unlike any I had ever felt before. *Was that the rainbow I'd been chasing since I was a child? No, this had to be better than any Oz I could imagine.*

Angel's words flooded my mind. *What would I do for this high? What wouldn't I do for it again?* I was hooked. I knew I was so damned hooked. I would do anything for this feeling. I tried to lift my eyelids, but couldn't even be bothered. I floated in serene blackness and tried to figure out how I could possibly get my next fix of this drug. I would do anything. I knew I would.

Chapter One

PRESENT DAY

I'd been shot for him. Okay, well, not just for him, but still. Nearly three months had gone by without a word from him. Not that we'd really left on good terms. I set the letter down, not wanting to read the rest of it. *Fucking letter, who even writes letters to people anymore?* My emotions were barreling out of control.

Three months. I'd known having something with Lachlan was doomed. But I hadn't realized just how much his absence would affect me. He was forced on me because Cannon said so, and if Cannon said so, then that was law. Or so I allowed him to believe. *Yeah, whatever helps you sleep at night, Addison.*

How'd my life gotten so messed up and complicated? *Well, had you not been a messed-up druggie, gotten in a shit ton of trouble with that dirt bag drug dealer, maybe you wouldn't be in this mess.* I groaned. My eyes slid over to the small end table where I set the letter.

Oh! I know, I just won't read the rest of it. Then it's like it never has to happen. My thoughts immediately went to Lachlan and the passion we'd shared. Then to his betrayal. He'd killed all of those people without so much of a thought. I gritted my teeth. *Could you really leave him to die, Addison?*

I closed my eyes and, like it had over the past three months, his face greeted me. The painted hard lines of his rugged face. His hair shaggy and often falling in his eyes. His piercing blue eyes, offset by his light-brown locks. His beard never quite gone but never really clean-shaven. His smile that was wicked and knowing. The tattoos that covered his arms and parts of his chest. The man was so delicious and, holy crap, how he'd made me feel.

My eyes flew open and landed right on the damn letter. No matter how he'd hurt me, no matter how mad I was, no matter any of it, I couldn't ignore him if he needed help. I picked up the letter and read.

Addison,
I know a letter is archaic, but when you read this, you will understand. I don't know how to start this, but if you're reading this, I am either dead or missing. Let's hope it is the latter shall we?

Cannon sent me on a mission that would erase one more of the favors I owed him. The crime rates in Atlanta have been on the rise and Cannon was sure a rogue group of turned pushers escaped the explosion. He asked me not to involve you. I am doing just that. Well, if you're reading this, I must be in some shit.

This letter is a safeguard. I need you to come find me. I know things didn't end well with us, but I hope you can forgive me right now, because I need you. I have included the address to my condo. That's the best place to start. Call Theo and Gen to help, but Addison, do not call Cannon. That is the whole reason for this letter. He has you monitored at your apartment.

If I am dead, please know I wish I could apologize to you, Addison. I wish I could have been the man you needed me to be. The one you deserved.

Lachlan O'Brian

I did the only thing I could. I threw the letter down as though it were constructed of thirteen pit vipers. *What the fuck is that? I mean really? I am a pusher! Not a miracle worker! And then that apology?* It didn't make my heart flutter. No, really, it didn't. *Shit!* I walked over to my cell phone.

What the hell am I doing? I couldn't call anyone. Cannon kept tabs on me, even in my apartment. I closed my eyes, trying to calm down. I needed to checklist this.

One, get out of the apartment. Two, call Theo. Three, think about calling Gen. Four, don't call Gen. Five, avoid Cannon. I opened my eyes and walked over to the letter. Picking it up, I scanned it again. I had to steel my heart. I couldn't make a decision based on the wildly beating muscle in my chest.

Damn Lachlan. Damn me for falling for him. I would never do it again. I would help him because he needed me. But, my heart would never again get in the middle. What's that saying? This wasn't personal, it was business. I closed my eyes. I pictured a cage, placed my tattered heart inside of it, locked it, and tossed away the key. Never again would I allow myself to fall for that Vampire. Normally, I lived by the "never say never" school of thought, but this time I really, really meant NEVER.

I grabbed my keys and stuffed the letter in my pocket, leaving my apartment in a hurry. I was in so much of a rush I very nearly ran over poor Mrs. Cho. Her paper bag that had to have been filled to the top with oranges exploded, causing the round fruit to go careening off in just about every conceivable direction.

"Oh my gosh! Mrs. Cho, I am so sorry!" I exclaimed, steadying the poor woman.

"Assin! Oh no, my onges." The woman could never quite say my name correctly. It always sounded like a curse word.

"I'll get them," I assured her. I quickly wrangled up the oranges and walked them up to her apartment. When she opened the door I was greeted by the scents of whatever she and Mr. Cho were cooking. The air was heavy with sautéed onions and spices that seemed to salt my tongue.

I placed the armload of oranges on her kitchen table. A small, white card caught my eye. I think I just stood there blinking at it. No. Freaking. Way. I reached for it. Maybe I was seeing things. On one side there was an ornate etching of two initials. CB. I could feel my face heating with anger. *Just what the hell is his card doing here?*

"Um, Mrs. Cho. How do you know Cannon Blackwood?" I tried to go for a nonchalant tone, but it only came of as accusatory.

"Oh da nice man came over. He want to help us redo kitchen. He nice man. Pretty man. I tell him you need man," she said, picking up the oranges and placing them in an ornately decorated bowl. Wait. What?

She told him I needed a what?

"Mrs. Cho! You can't tell people I need a man! I'm fine." I cannot believe Cannon came here, and I cannot believe she told him I needed a man.

"Oh no, Assin, you do need man. He come yeserday. I give him your number," she informed me in the same tone that someone would use when ordering a pizza. *What the hell is going on? Am I in some sort of alternate universe?* I was afraid to ask her anything else for fear of her saying she gave him a key or nude photos of me, so I just nodded and told her sorry again for nearly knocking her down.

"You slow down, Assin." Her tone was just as bright as her smile. She had a smile that crinkled the corners of her eyes, nearly causing them to close completely.

"Yes, ma'am," I replied as I left.

Lachlan's apartment was on the other side of town from mine, so it took me longer to run there, even with my extraordinary speed. I knew the part of town where Lachlan lived from my drug days. I knew nearly every part of Atlanta from that time.

When I got to the address, which was just off of Peachtree Street, I couldn't really do anything other than gawk at the huge, ostentatious building. *This can't be right.* I pulled the letter out of my pocket and scanned the address. *Yeah, this is it.* The tall building screamed money. I wasn't too sure what I was expecting, but this sure as shit wasn't it. I had no idea that Lachlan had that kind of money. That fact didn't really change anything, but now I wouldn't feel bad making him buy me donuts.

I pulled my cell phone out of my pocket and dialed Theo.

"Hey, chickadee. What's good?" Even over the phone, Theo's tone felt like a warm hug. His voice seemed to calm me appreciably.

"Hey, Theo, um, I could use your help with something."

"Care to elaborate?"

I bit my lower lip, trying to think of something to tell him.

"Addison, you there?" he asked.

"Yeah, sorry. Um, can you meet me at Lachlan's?" I asked in a rushed tone.

He made a noise much like someone spitting out a drink. I tried not to roll my eyes at the phone, I really did. But, it didn't work.

"What the hell are you doing there? I thought you said the next time you saw him … What were your words? Oh yeah, now I remember. You said the next time you saw him, it would be to cut his head off with his dick."

Oh my. Had I said that? No, not me. Okay, maybe I said it.

"Theo, I never said that," I informed him.

"Really? You gunna go there?" he asked, clearly attempting not to laugh.

"Ugh, okay fine. Will you just get here?" I scoffed.

"Okay, okay, keep your panties on. And I mean that."

Was he snickering?

I opened my mouth to give him an exquisitely thought-out and witty retort, but I heard the telltale click of an ended call. I scowled at the phone.

I returned my attention to the oversized building. *Now or never, Addison. Wait, is never an option? Is that on the table? Uh, no.* I walked into the building and paused after only a few steps. The lobby was massive. There was white and gold marble laid throughout the expansive space. There were accents of black and gold everywhere. This was the kind of place I would expect from Cannon. But Lachlan? No way.

"Ma'am?" A tall Hispanic man jarred me to attention.

"Oh, I'm sorry. I have just never been here before," was all I could manage.

"Can I help you find something?" He had a tone of sweetness to him.

"Oh, um, maybe. I am looking for apartment, wait condo, number 2098."

Lachlan hadn't left me a key or anything so I had no way of actually accessing his place.

"Oh, that's Mr. Lachlan's penthouse. Come with me." He began to make his way to an ornate black desk that ran along the entire north side of the building. He turned to face me.

"I'll be right back." He opened a door and stepped through it. The door shut behind him with a soft click. A few moments later the same man reappeared behind the large desk. I spared a glance to the man's nametag; it read Jose.

"Okay, can I have your ID?" he asked in a brisk tone as he nearly pounded on the poor keyboard. I rummaged around in my pocket for the required documentation, then handed him my driver's license and waited.

"Oh, Ms. Fitzpatrick! I am so sorry, I did not know it was you!" His voice was shaking. He acted as though he had made some egregious error. All I could manage besides the dumb look on my face was to stand there blinking at him.

"Uh, me?" I asked, somewhat stupefied. *What did he mean by he didn't know it was me?*

"Mr. Lachlan's wife. He said if you ever came here, I was to give you all of his keys and access to everything." I think I just gaped at him. Mouth open and eyes wide. *Did he just say wife? As in married?*

"Uh, um, what?" was all I could choke out. What the fuck could I really say to that? Had he told them that? *I'm going to kill him. I'm going to take the nearest fork I find and stab him to death with it.*

"Here are the keys he left for you. He said you are to have access to everything just as he does. You need to take that elevator to the twentieth floor and then turn right," he explained. I took the keys and blinked up at him.

"Have a wonderful day, Ms. Fitzpatrick." He said, clearly dismissing me. I turned and stumbled to the elevator. What in the name of all that is holy was he thinking?

I whirled to face the desk and shouted, "I'm not his wife!" *Oh shit, I did not just yell that.* Everyone turned to face me. I felt my cheeks warm and turned back to the freaking elevator.

"Damned Vampire makes me crazy and he's not even here!" I mumbled under my breath, knowing no one could hear.

Jose had the nerve to just wave at me as though I were simple-minded. I scowled at him. *Men are stupid.* Vampire or human, they all had to be dropped on their heads at birth.

I turned my attention back to the elevator. I pressed the up button and waited. And waited. Where the crap was the elevator coming back from, outer space? It took all of ten minutes for the damned thing to finally get to the ground floor.

Thank goodness the elevator didn't take as long to get to the twentieth floor, or I would have had to beat someone. The elevator was much like the rest of the building, ornate and expensive looking. I guess I shouldn't be shocked that he had money, but damn, I would have no idea how to live like that. I had to focus my thoughts, because my emotions were a hair shy of pressing the crazy button.

I paused in front of his door. Maybe I could just turn away. I wouldn't have to face any of this. I closed my eyes and drew in a deep gulp of air. Why did I feel like I needed to run hella far away? I felt like this was one situation that I may not make it out of. I had no idea if it was foreboding or me just trying to avoid seeing a man who broke my heart. When I opened my eyes, the door was still there and whatever Lachlan needed me to find would lay just beyond it. That was the going thought anyway. Lachlan needed me. He needed help. And no matter how pissy I was, I had to help him if I could.

You're a badass pusher, Addison, start acting like it!

I slid the small gold key in the slot and turned the doorknob.

Chapter Two

I didn't make it far into the condo, apartment, thingy, before a loud beeping noise began blaring. I whirled to face the abrasive shrilling beeping. It was a fucking alarm. *Wonderful.* I had no idea what the code was. I hadn't been given the damn thing. The small white box hanging on the wall was wailing and I had no clue how to make it stop. I pressed a small button that said cancel. Yeah, that did a whole big bunch of nothing.

Shit! I was going to have to smash the thing. Oh! I typed in the apartment number. Nothing happened. There was a clock counting down and it was now at twenty. I was going to have to defuse this thing like a bomb. When Jose handed me the keys there was a card with it. It had to have the code on it or I was screwed.

The small ivory card had four numbers on it: zero, two, one, four. I quickly mashed each of the numbers into the keypad. The alarm went silent. I just gaped at it. It took a moment for it to really sink in, but I knew those numbers. I had known them my whole freaking life. The stinking code was my birthday. I was going to have to file that away in the mental Rolodex of things I would have to address when next I saw Mister Vampire. Because if I spent too much time thinking about it, I would make a much bigger deal about it than it was.

I returned my attention to the very dark apartment, putting a hand out in front of me to try to find a wall. When my palm met the cool, smooth plaster, I stepped lightly forward, letting my fingers run along the wall. It was the middle of the day, so I was guessing Lachlan had some type of daytime shade that covered his windows. Smart for him, but a broken ankle waiting to happen for me.

Finally, my hand found a light switch. I flicked it on. I blinked a few times, giving my eyes time to adjust to the new, intrusive light. Then, the expansiveness of his home hit me. House seemed to be too small of a word. This place was massive, and pristinely cleaned. The floors were all a black marble with veins of gold. *I bet I could eat off of these floors, the place is so clean.* I had the instant urge to pour cereal and milk all over the floor just to create a little mischief.

Wait. I paused as a strange thought hit me. Why the hell would he want to stay in my shithole of an apartment when he had this? I shook my head, trying to rid myself of anything other than why I was here. I had to find something that led me to Lachlan.

I walked down the short hallway that opened up into the large living room. The kitchen was just off to the right of the short hallway. *Hmm, does he actually have food? Or blood?* Okay, I mean, I couldn't not look! His kitchen was what culinary experts dream of. I would have no idea what to do with it, well, other than make a cup of noodles. But it sure was pretty. The floor was hardwood. It was so dark it was nearing black. The counters were an off-white mixed with gray. The cabinets were the same color as the floor, but they were also glass and backlit with a faint amber light. Well, there were dishes. I searched the large room for a refrigerator. No stainless steel, but there was a large wooden door that matched the rest of the decor. I walked over and opened it.

The refrigerator was completely empty except for one thing. In the middle sat a bag of unopened, chocolate-covered donuts. I smiled. I couldn't help it. I reached for the bag. I mean, it was almost like a peace offering. Who was I to turn it down? I opened the bag and popped one of the goodies into my mouth. He hadn't left me milk. But, they were still donuts.

"Seriously. You would find the only food in this place."

I very nearly peed my pants. I knew who the voice belonged to, but damn, it scared the tar out of me.

"Oh my damn! Theo, you almost had a cleanup on aisle three situation on your hands," I gasped, placing a hand over my now racing heart.

"Ha ha ha, okay I'm glad you held it in." He walked over to the bar and sat down, pulling the small blue bag closer and reaching in. He took a bite, then narrowed his eyes at me.

"Addison, come on, these are nothing compared to Krispy Kreme."

"Well, they're better than no donuts. And I see you managed to finish it anyway."

He rolled his eyes, but was smiling. He had that kind of infectious smile that left me grinning ear to ear.

"Why are we here, chickadee? Where's Lachlan?" he asked, looking around. I swallowed the new lump in my throat and reached into my pocket to retrieve the letter. I pushed it toward him. His brow furrowed and his mouth was set in a hard white line.

"Cliff notes?"

I bit my lip and shook my head. He needed

everything, not a summarization. Plus, I didn't trust myself to explain without my emotions getting the better of me. I saw in his face the moment he realized this was a serious situation. His eyes shut and he put the letter down. One might think by his drawn features he was calm. But, I knew Theo. His hands were white knuckled by how hard he was holding onto the counter.

"Why didn't he ask for help? He has never gone and done something like this without me and Gen." His tone was even, but there was an edge to it.

"I don't know. But, he told me to call you and look here." I wanted to press him and ask more but he looked incensed, so I waited for him to tell me. He stood up and began to pace. His shiny head was dotted with sweat. Lachlan was his best friend. I hated for him to be upset. Hell, that letter had nearly toppled me over, and I hadn't known Lachlan as long as Theo did.

"Addison, all he told me was that he needed space and time."

Space and time? What did that even mean?

"Space and time from what?"

His deep-brown eyes flew to meet my blue ones. Then it hit me. Space and time away from me. The knowledge hit me like a physical blow.

This whole time, I had been focusing on me. Focusing on what he did to me. I never once stopped to think about how he felt. I ripped our bond away without a second thought. Without a single word of protest. Not that it would have mattered with Cannon.

"Addison, I'm not blaming you. He is a big boy and can make his own decisions. It just hurts he didn't say anything."

I nodded at his words. I couldn't trust myself to even speak. Lachlan could be dead and it could all be because of me.

"Have you called Gen?" he asked, running a large hand over his jaw. Which I now realized was covered in stubble.

"No. I wanted to have something to tell her before she lost her shit."

"Good idea."

"I have no idea where to start looking though." I was kind of at a loss. I didn't know Lachlan like Theo did. Then again, I knew him in the Kama Sutra sense. That thought caused heat to flood to my face.

"I guess we should start with his office."

"He has an office?" I asked.

"Uh yeah, why is that so surprising?"

"I guess I thought he just had a lair."

He raised an eyebrow at me and busted out in guffaws.

Between gulps of air and whoops of laughter he managed to say, "Okay, come, speedy pants. Let's get to work."

Three hours. We scoured that damned place for three freaking hours and found his laptop and not much else. Theo sat on the pristine white couch in the middle of the living room. The infernal thing looked like a mid-evil torture device. It was white leather studded with white buttons. I preened a little bit thinking about how much better my beast of a couch was.

I let Theo do his thing and went to look around the only room we hadn't looked at yet. Lachlan's bedroom. My heart rate picked up at the thought of going in there.

I pushed the door open. There was a huge bed in the center of the room and the room was utterly black. The windows were still covered, so I had to find the light switch. But flicking it on didn't help. Everything in the room was black, including the walls. It was like a cave. I wasn't sure what I expected, but black as a cave wasn't it. I walked over to the massive bed, trying desperately not to jump in and roll around like a dog.

I touched the satin sheets. No, there was no reason for me to do this. But, I couldn't help it. His bed wasn't made. The sheets and blankets lay in a mound atop the mattress. I traced a finger along the silky fabric until I stood at the head of his bed. I slid my hand to rest on his pillow. How long had it been since he slept here? Had he been alone? I wanted to kick myself for even caring. Did it smell like him? I bit my bottom lip, hoping that the slight pain would break the trance this man still held over me. For shit's sake, he wasn't even here and he still had an iron hold on me. I tasted blood. That seemed to shatter the spell. I shook my head, only to realize nothing would get him out of my thoughts.

I laid down. *Just what the hell am I doing?* I flipped over until my face was buried in his pillow and breathed in deep. I could smell him. His sharp scent of Old Spice mixed with a scent that was all him. It was utterly indescribable. I slid my hands under his pillow. My fingers brushed something soft. I grasped the foreign object and pulled it out, then just gaped at the scrap of material. I mean, fully open mouth and possibly even with drool trickling down.

"Oh, you have got to be shitting me," I said out loud in an exasperated tone. The bastard had a pair of my underwear! I scowled at the small, pink-lace-covered panties. The scowl didn't last long as I just couldn't help but smile. I shoved Lachlan's prize back under the pillow and stood up abruptly.

I punched the pillow. Mature, I know. But, damn him. Damn him for making me feel whatever this was. And damn him for not being here. I yanked my hand from the soft material as though it were on fire. I scanned the room again and my eyes landed on a bedside table. It, too, was black. Though, unlike most black furniture, this was ornately carved with curls and twists of wood. It was utterly stunning. The time the artist spent on the drawers alone, sheesh, it had to be years. I couldn't help but caress the slick wood. A jolt went through me, causing a shiver to wrack my whole body. I slid the top drawer open and looked at its contents. I stared.

There was a small, red booklet. Okay, this wasn't an address book, it was a journal. Etched into the creamy red leather was an ornate L. I picked it up and opened it. The first date was about a month before we met. I fanned through to the last date. It was two days after he broke our bonds. I shook at the remembered pain.

"Find something good to read?"

I screamed and my hand flew to cover my heart as though that would somehow slow the galloping horse that took over my heartbeat.

"Jesus, Mary and Joseph. Are you trying to give me a heart attack?" I scolded between gasps of air.

He just laughed and shook his head. I narrowed my eyes at him.

"What?" I questioned as I eyed him.

"Oh nothing, Miss I'm Over Lachlan. And when did you become so religious?" he chided as he walked into the room.

I tried to give him my best pithy retort but nothing came out.

I did the only thing I could. I threw my hands up in supplication and groaned.

"Okay, fine, maybe I'm not 100% over him."

"Praise to God she finally speaks the truth!"

I rolled my eyes at him.

"Did you find anything?" I asked as I realized I still held Lachlan's journal. I did the only intelligent thing I could, the one thing someone who is totally over a guy would do. I slipped it in the back of the waistband my shorts and pulled my shirt to cover it. Either Theo hadn't seen the motion or he ignored it.

"Yeah, I have his tablet and laptop. Only one small problem."

I raised an eyebrow at him.

"Password protected. And, I'm willing to bet that

Brent set up the protections on both."

"Ugh, really. Okay, so now what?" I groaned. Why couldn't this be simple? Like, a letter stating where he was and how to find him. Oh no, that shit would be too damned easy.

"We have to get Brent to bypass his password settings. But, there is a small issue there as well."

I motioned for him to continue as I was attempting to save him from the current stream of vitriol I knew would come spewing forth if I opened my mouth.

"Yeah, Brent works for Cannon now. I can email or text him but…"

"But, what?"

"But, I don't honestly know where Brent is." He wouldn't meet my eyes.

"Wait. What? You lost Brent?! How the fuck did you lose a nearly four-hundred-pound white man?" I knew my tone was incredulous but how the hell did he lose Brent? The man never saw the sun. Hell, he wasn't just white, I think he glowed.

"I didn't lose him. Cannon has him tucked away. And besides, what am I, his keeper?"

"Yes! You are!" I nearly yelled.

He just scoffed in reply.

"Can we just take the computer to a computer fix it

shop? Maybe they can…" I trailed off at his expression. I let out a long breath.

"I'm going to have to go see Cannon, aren't I?" I moaned. I didn't want to do that. Lachlan asked me not to and seeing Cannon always did funny things to me. He had this strange ability to very nearly cause my panties to melt and leave me panting.

"Chickadee, I don't see that you really have another choice. Want me to go with you?"

I shook my head.

"No."

I really didn't want Theo to see the effect Cannon had on me.

"Hey, Addison, time is short. I think you need to get going," he said, walking out of Lachlan's bedroom. I followed behind him, pausing at the doorway and flicking the light off without looking back.

"Do you need a ride?" Theo asked half-heartedly. Clearly, he expected the answer.

"No, I need to clear my head. But, I'll let you know what goes down," I informed him.

I turned down the hall that led to the front door. I reached for the knob and paused at Theo's ringing tone calling from the living room.

"Chickadee! You want me to bring you that book

you got stuffed in your shorts, you know, so you don't have to run with it?"

Shit. I felt my face heat. I felt like I had just got caught with my hand in the cookie jar.

"No. I got it," I called back, shutting the door.

All I heard was Theo's deep laughter echoing through the hallway.

I had the sinking feeling I was going from one cave to the next. Just more shit for me to wade through. *Great. Just freaking wonderful.*

Chapter Three

I f I had to make a list of the people I didn't want to see, Cannon would be in the top five. I thought briefly about calling him or even trying to call out to him mentally, but, knowing him, he wouldn't help me unless it was in person anyway. Cannon was just such a joy. Yeah, a joy like going to the bathroom and realizing there's no toilet paper but, instead, there is sandpaper, covered in poison ivy.

Normally when I ran, I tried to push myself to the brink. To the point where I thought I would go flying apart, just beyond that. But I was stalling this run. It took me nearly twenty minutes to get to the obnoxiously large building. On a day where I wasn't avoiding him, it should have taken me about five.

I was procrastinating, and I knew it. It had been a few months since the last time I saw him. In fact, it was the day he rebound me. *Wait.* I was mad at him. He had gone to Mr. and Mrs. Cho's just to keep an extra eye on me. I sighed. There it was. I could do pissed off at him. I held on to that emotion and walked into the building.

I pushed the button for the elevator and prepared to wait. Surprisingly, it popped open right away. I smiled and stepped in. Then paused. *Wait. What if this was a bad omen. I mean, I have the worst luck with elevators.* I was losing my mind. I slid my card in the slot and pressed the button that would take me to see Cannon.

The sun had been setting when I ran here. I hadn't realized just how long I had been at Lachlan's. I just hoped Cannon was awake — considering how early it was I wasn't sure — and willing to not give me shit about helping. The elevator dinged and the doors slid open. I strode up to the frosted glass doors and, just as I was about to knock, I paused, looking at the clearly visible latch on the door just to my right. I just gaped at it. The door was open. Now, that was odd. Where the hell was that Santa-looking bastard who always opened the damn door? *Do I knock? Or do I just go in like I own the place?* I almost laughed, as I always strode into a place as if I owned it. *Pfft, like there is really any other choice.*

I placed a hand on the cool glass and pushed slightly. The door eased open and I slid in. My heart was racing. I had never known anyone to just leave this door open. Something felt wrong. Terribly wrong. I paused, looking around, trying to survey the dark entrance-way. I crept down the hallway and looked inside the white room. The room was cast in a soft purple glow as the sun had just set and night was making its first appearance. This had been the room where I had to make that deal with the devil. The deal that intertwined my life with both Cannon and Lachlan. The deal I felt sure would be the last nail in my coffin.

A soft moan drew my attention away from the white room. It was a moan of pain. I could now hear the rush of blood in my ears from my erratic heartbeat. I heard a slap of skin and another moan. I ran into the main room.

Of the things I was expecting to see, the scene that played out before me wasn't even on the same god-damned planet. In fact, take the fucking list of things and set that son of a bitch on fire.

Cannon sat on a chair. And straddling him was a very naked woman. Her skin was the color of melted chocolate and looked just as smooth. Her hair was cut so short it was nearly buzzed. But, she had a head and long sculpted neck that could pull it off. Cannon's fangs were embedded in the woman's neck. His eyes flicked to mine, nearly black. The corners of his lips twitched. *Is he smiling at me?*

I tried to look away. I really tried. But I couldn't make myself move, not one single inch. I had the sudden urge to toss this woman to the floor and take her place. Wait, what? No, I certainly did NOT have that image playing over and over in my mind!

Cannon released his mouth from the woman's throat and she whimpered in protest. Finally, blessedly, I was able to turn away. I heard the sound of movement and the rustling of clothes.

"Addison. What a pleasant surprise."

I turned to see Cannon with black silk pants on. Oh thank God, because had he not had pants on I may have … Oh shit, I didn't even want to think about that. My eyes clearly had a mind of their own and flicked to the enormous bulge in his pants.

Shit! I immediately slid my gaze to something less mesmerizing.

His eyes grew dark. I felt heat rush past my foggy brain, past my thudding heart, right to my now damp sex. *Great.* My eyes shifted to the woman. Who, by the way, was still very nude and staring daggers at me. Okay, so I had always been a "love the one you're with" kinda chick. For the most part, I had always been attracted to men. That all having been said, this woman was exquisite. She stood about the size of an

Amazonian princess. I'm talking the "I need snu-snu" kinda woman. She stood nearly six-foot tall, at least. She was slim in the waist, full in the hips and breasts. Everywhere else she was all muscle. There was no way she would be as fast as me, but damn, she looked like she could fight.

She sauntered over to Cannon and I honestly couldn't help but watch her full breasts sway as she moved. Mine would never be that full without some major plastic surgery and divine intervention. And, something told me the big guy upstairs, if there was such a dude, had better things to do than increase the size of my bust.

The woman paused at Cannon's side and wrapped an arm around his shoulders. Her high cheekbones shone in the full light of the room. She looked like a full-on goddess. Here I stood, a whopping five foot two in ratty shorts and a too-ratty old tank top that I may or may not have slept in. My blonde hair sat atop my head in a mess with loose curls falling down. I looked like Little Orphan Annie. Yet, Cannon never took his eyes off me. He did, however, seem amused at whatever the expression was that was plastered on my face. If I were to set an egg on it, it would likely fry in moments. My throat was dry.

"Uh, um," was all my rattled brain could come up with. *Pathetic, Addison.*

"Will she be joining us?" the tall woman purred. Her palm moved to the front of Cannon's pants. She stroked him once before he grabbed her hand. His eyebrow went up in question. Wait, what? Was he wondering if I would ...

"Oh, hell no!" I nearly tripped over the words trying to get them out as quickly as possible. If I had shaken my head in the negative any more it might have popped off all together.

Cannon shrugged.

"Leave us." His tone was low, Eastern European accent becoming slightly more pronounced.

"Shall I wait up-" Her smooth voice was cut off by Cannon's deadly tone.

"I'm done with you, leave."

She and I both knew by his edged voice that he was done. She strode forward. Walking past me, she whispered, "Whore."

I have a bad attitude on the best of days. Today had not been a good day. I looked at Cannon and held up a finger indicating I would be back in a moment.

It only took a second to run past her and trip her. She made a glorious thud as she fell to the floor. Smiling, I once again stood in front of Cannon. Distantly, I heard her muffled curse. Her tone held a note of embarrassment. She had no idea I'd done it as I heard her rush out of the condo.

"Was that necessary?" Cannon questioned as he strode over to his bar.

I gave his question genuine thought before I replied, "Well, no, it wasn't. But, damn, it was satisfying."

He smiled. Not one of his all teeth, "I'm a predator" smiles. But, a genuinely amused smile. I wouldn't go so far as to say it was happy, as I didn't think Cannon was capable of happy. He looked beautiful in that moment. Not a monster dressed up in the suit of a man.

"As amusing as it was to watch you play with my food, why are you here, Addison?" He walked over to the white leather couch and sat down. He motioned for me to sit with him. Hesitating for only a moment, I went over and sat. He still had no shirt on, and his nearly black hair was bound back at the base of his neck. But, my attention was on his bared chest and torso. He was sculpted. This man couldn't have been created like a normal man. He surely had to have been painstakingly carved. I licked my lips without thought.

"Do that again and I will pin you against the wall

and drive so deep inside of you that you won't know where I end and you begin," he informed me in such a tone that indicated he wasn't joking in the least.

Holy shit. I now had flashes of him doing just that. Had the room just gotten hot? Maybe the A/C got turned off. Or a fire. Did Santa or whatever his name was turn the fire on?

"Um, Cannon, I need to find Brent." It was a rasp, but damn, it was all I could manage.

"Why?" His eyes sparked as though he already knew the answer. *Damn him.*

"Cannon, get out of my head." I tried to blank my thoughts but it was too little too late at that point. Who the hell thought it was a great idea for a vampire to be able to read my thoughts?

"Do tell me, Addison." He was grinning. *Smug bastard.*

"I need Brent to help me unlock a computer." I really wanted to avoid telling him about Lachlan.

"Whose computer, Addison?" *Fuck me.* Lying to him really wasn't an option.

Okay, it was, but I wasn't willing to accept the consequences.

"Lachlan's." His eyebrows shot up and his smile widened.

"The plot thickens. Tell me what my dear brother is up to?" His tone held a note of amusement. There was no getting through this without doing the one thing Lachlan asked me not to do. I didn't have a choice. I needed Cannon, or at least for him to tell me the location of Brent. So, I told him.

Cannon listened intently. He stroked his stubble-covered chin while I was talking.

"So, you want my help saving my bother?" he asked in a cocky as hell tone.

"No. I want Brent's help. Cannon, I know you really don't care about your bother."

His hand flew over the gaping hole where his black heart should have been and he explained in mock hurt, "Addison, you wound me. Though I had wondered why I hadn't heard from him in a week."

"Cannon. Please. You're the one who sent him on this mission in the first place. Doesn't that mean anything to you?" It was a whisper. I didn't want to beg.

His only response was a shrug. God, why did he hate his brother so much? I'd give anything to know where my brother, Aaron, was.

"How about a deal?" he asked, seeming a little too pleased with himself. That scared the crap out of me.

I narrowed my eyes at him.

"This is a big favor. You'll have to owe me two additional favors."

Of course I would. Cannon never did anything unless he got something from it. That would bring my total up to four. At this rate, he would own my ass until I was toothless and in a nursing home.

"Oh-" he added almost as an afterthought. "You also must let me help you every step of the way."

"Wait! What? Why?" There was no fucking way. Not just no, but hell no.

"These are the terms, Addison. Take them or leave them."

"He's your brother! I mean, don't you care at all about what happens to him?"

He shrugged. That's the answer I got. What a fucking monster. I laughed. I couldn't help it. I kept doing it, kept thinking he was human. He wasn't and never would be again. I could think about the options until I was blue in the face and it wouldn't change a goddamned thing.

I needed Brent. Therefore, I needed Cannon. I knew he had some reason for wanting to "help" me, because he couldn't care less about his brother. Cannon never did anything just to be helpful. He had an ulterior motive; I just didn't know what it was.

I tried to think of another solution. Maybe just having him add more favors, but I knew the thought was fruitless. It was this or nothing. That was how Cannon worked.

Much like seven years ago, I gave him the same answer as before, in the same resigned and defeated tone.

"Yes."

Chapter Four

S o, now that I'm in this situation, how about you tell me what the mission was that you sent him on?" Okay, even I sounded snarky to myself. But damn, I think I deserved to cop a little bit of an attitude.

"After he killed all of the turned pushers, I would have thought the crime around Atlanta would have gone down, but it didn't. This led me to believe that some of the pushers escaped. I sent Lachlan to find them and eradicate them."

He spoke so nonchalantly about killing people that it honestly disturbed me. Though this "reason" he spoke of seemed a little too easy.

"Cannon, they're people, you know. I just don't understand how you and Lachlan could kill them so easily."

Maybe the years of not being human really had killed any bit of humanity they had left.

"Because, Addison, they are dangerous. They could kill hundreds of humans and, with each day that passes, the stronger they become. They don't have enough control to not kill when they feed. Nor do they differentiate when picking a victim."

"What do you mean?"

"My feeders feed me of their own free will. While I cannot trance, it's not one of my skills, I can be very persuasive. These abominations can't do that. Well, if they can, they certainly don't. They feed with no care. This means even from children."

His words hung in the air like frozen drops of acid wanting to come in contact with bare skin so they could burn and sting more than they already did. They were killing children. Just the thought nearly sent me running to the bathroom.

I felt his cool hand just under my chin. He drew my face up to meet his dispassionate eyes.

"Hate me, condemn me and think of me as a monster, but, Addison I have my reasons for the things I do. Especially when they involve children."

His tone was so firm. Where the hell was he when I was a child? Where was he when I was being hurt every god-damned day?

"Oh, Addison, I wish I had known you then. I would have done more than save you."

My eyes stung with tears that I refused to let spill.

I blinked rapidly and tore my gaze from his. I couldn't look at him for one more moment for fear of tumbling head long into something I wasn't sure I could survive.

"Cannon, I need Brent. He's the one who set up the security system on Lachlan's laptop and tablet. It's all we have to go on right now." I had to force the words out through my too-dry and clenched throat.

"Do you have the laptop with you?" He asked as he stood up from the couch.

"No, Theo has it."

"I'll text him Brent's address to have him meet us there," he said, walking down the hallway. I was about to protest him coming, but then I remembered our deal. I was going to have to bite my tongue quite a bit.

"Where are you going?" I had no idea why even asked.

"To get dressed. Would you like to help me?" There was an amused tone to his voice.

"Um, no thanks." *Only if I can use my teeth.* I didn't say that last bit, but my libido sure as shit wanted to. All I heard was his soft, deep laughter echoing behind him as he disappeared around the corner to the stairs.

Wonderful. Just fucking wonderful.

Cannon was a manipulative rat bastard. He moved

Brent into the apartment building next to mine. I mean, for shit's sake. We pulled up to see Theo leaning against the building, shaking his head. I knew exactly what he was thinking and I agreed one hundred percent. I could honestly throttle Cannon. I let my eyes flick to him. The ass fuck had this cocky grin just plastered on his perfect damn face. *What is that sound?* It was a deep rumbling, almost vibrating noise. *Wait. Oh, hell no.*

"Are you seriously laughing at me right now?" I was incredulous. What was once just a twitch of his mouth turned into a big broad smile that crinkled the soft skin at the corners of his dark eyes.

"Addison. You're just so cute when you imagine yourself strangling me." His words were amused and that only seemed to piss me off even more.

I tried my damndest to think of something witty but all I could say was, "You're infuriating and I think I hate you." It didn't surprise me he was reading my thoughts, but I needed to find a way to guard myself against him.

"Come, Addison, your Theo is waiting, and please inform him I haven't bitten you, so there will be no need to stake me through the balls," he said calmly as he exited the car.

I rolled my eyes at his back but couldn't help the grin that appeared at the thought of Theo's described actions.

"Addison," Theo called abruptly as I was getting out of the car. His words caused me to lose concentration and the toe of my shoe caught the lip of the sidewalk. I took two large steps forward with hopes of righting my trajectory and preventing myself from falling, but I had no time to even react. I flew forward and the ground rushed up to meet me.

Strong arms encircled my waist. I was only about an inch away from faceplanting into the concrete. The cool body seemed to vibrate behind me. Cannon pulled me closer so I could stand unassisted. I felt his words brush lightly against my skin long before my rattled brain registered them as a sound.

"See, Addison. What would you do without me?"

He was way too close. I needed to get away from him. Like thirteen states away. Like half a country, at least. I shifted, not so subtly indicating that I wanted him to release me. He did, but in such a way that led me to believe he was doing so on his terms and his terms alone. That was Cannon. He may do something I wanted but he would damn sure make me know he did it because he wanted to, not because I wanted him to.

"Sorry," I said, looking at Theo, "And thank you," I called to Cannon. I tried like hell to make it sound like a cuss word.

"Can I talk to you for a moment, Addison?" Theo asked in a tone that was clearly annoyed. I walked over to him and we headed a few paces off to the right of the all-brick building.

"Addison! What the fuck is he doing here? Did you forget that little tidbit in Lachlan's letter? You know, about not getting Cannon involved?" His words were hushed and coming in rapid fire.

"I know! Cannon didn't really give me much of a choice! Trust me, if I could do this without having him here, I would." My tone was a little harsh. I hadn't meant to sound like such a bitch, but I was already in a shit mood.

"I'm sorry. I should have assumed that you had a reason for him being here. My bad." He sounded genuinely sorry, and that just made me feel like crap. I wanted to say something, but had no idea what words would help.

"Come on, chickadee, let's get this over with," he said, breaking the expanse of silence.

It was Cannon who now leaned against the wall waiting. The pose looked forced on him, whereas with

Theo it was natural. For once, Cannon looked out of his element. This didn't soften my feelings toward him in the least though.

"If you two are finished bitching about me being here, we could just get this over with." Cannon's tone held an edge but no force. Theo looked surprised. I, however, knew even if we had gone a city block, Cannon would have still found a way to overhear anything we said.

I gestured at him with a flick of my wrist to go on and push the button. He rolled his eyes. An action I would have thought below him, but he did push the second button from the top.

"Hello?" Brent's tinny voice sounded from the small, brass-colored speaker box.

"It's Cannon." No explanation followed. The telltale buzz of the door unlocking sounded and Cannon pulled the door open. The building was identical to mine. The only difference was that the stairs were on the right side of the entrance and mine were on the left. We turned immediately to the first door on the left and saw Brent standing silhouetted in the light that was spilling out from his apartment.

Backlit or not, Brent looked horrific. His once-plum features were sunken in. His face seemed to simply hang on his head. He had been in excess of three hundred pounds the last time I saw him. Now, he was maybe half of that weight. He looked pale and haunted. I wanted nothing more in that moment than to hug him. Yes, he had gotten me shot. But, he was clearly going through hell.

I glanced to Theo, who looked exactly how I felt. As though we had abandoned him. And, I guess in a way, we had.

Finally, Brent looked up and met my eyes. His brown orbs that once squinted in his round face with every expression were now lifeless and dull.

"Uh. Hi, um, Brent," was all I could manage. Getting me shot or not, I hated seeing him like that.

"Oh, hi, Addison. Hey, Theo." God, even his voice was laced with pain.

"May we come in?" Cannon asked, clearly not caring a damn thing for Brent. I narrowed my eyes at him and opened my mouth to say something but was halted by Brent.

"Oh yeah, sorry. Come on in." He stepped out of the doorway. He was no longer backlit and I could see just what the last few months had truly done to him. He had lost so much weight that his clothes looked like giant trash bags that had to be secured by an overly large belt. His skin had not been as forgiving of his weight loss. His neck resembled that of a turkey.

As I stepped into his apartment, I realized that not everything about him had changed. His apartment was a wreck of old ramen noodle cups, loose papers, dirty clothes and other assorted things.

"Uh, sorry. I didn't know you guys were coming over or I would have picked the place up a bit," he replied to accusations that weren't voiced.

We all just stood there not really knowing what to say.

"Um. Not to be rude but why are you here?" he asked, seeming to be deliberately not looking at Cannon.

"It's kind of a long story," Theo replied, glancing at me.

I took that as my cue to explain about Lachlan. And I did.

After I explained the letter to Brent, his face fell. I, of course, left out some of the more intimate moments of the letter. Brent raised his hands to his face and ran them along his forehead, over his eyes, down his gaunt cheeks and along his scruff-covered jaw. His movements only seemed to highlight his declining physical state. His distress was the most emotion I had seen from him the entire time I had been here.

There was a protracted silence. We all just sat, staring at Brent. It would be easy to not care about him, but I didn't have it in me to hate him. Even if his actions had almost killed me.

"It will take a few minutes. Where's the laptop?" Bret's tone was resigned.

Theo held it up and replied, "I got it, boss. And the tablet."

"The tablet will take longer. Come on. Follow me to the back."

Theo and Brent left the cluttered room, leaving me and Cannon, alone. Oh goodie.

Ten or so minutes passed and I couldn't take it anymore. I got up and started picking some of the copious amounts of shit up. I hated feeling useless. I couldn't help but sneak glances at Cannon, who stood leaning against a wall. He was eyeing me and he looked amused. I rolled my eyes and continued. Then, abruptly, I turned to him.

"Why aren't you helping Brent?" My tone was harsh, but the question had been on the edge of my thoughts ever since I stepped foot in this place.

"I don't clean," he replied with an arch in his eyebrow.

"Cannon, that's not what I mean and you know it." He was being obtuse on purpose and it was pissing me off.

He sighed. The action surprised me. He didn't need to breathe; he was dead, thus sighing wasn't something he did.

"Addison, I have no idea where his sister is. All searches for the person who funded the drug Jack developed have dried up. I've tried to get Brent to tell both you and Theo where he was. I have even tried to get him to see Gen. He wouldn't hear of any of it. And I am not going to force him to see anyone he has no interest in seeing." He was telling the truth. Not just a half truth that benefitted him, but the whole, honest-to-god, truth. I couldn't speak. He really had cared enough about someone other than himself to try to help them. I couldn't help but wonder what was in it for him.

Cannon laughed low in his throat.

"What?" I asked, turning fully to him.

He pushed off the wall and walked toward me. Whenever Cannon came toward me, my instincts screamed at me to run the hell away. This was a predator and the last thing I wanted to look like was his prey. He walked up to me until his chest brushed my breasts. I stifled a shiver that his touch always seemed to induce. He put a finger under my chin and drew my gaze to his.

"I'm not human. But that, in no way, means I'm a monster." His voice was deep and dark. His finger trailed from my chin down my throat. I closed my eyes, trying not to enjoy his touch.

"Then tell me there is nothing in it for you. Tell me if Brent was better, it in no way helps you." I couldn't look at him. I could only concentrate on the feel of his cool finger tracing a line up and down on the large artery that ran along my neck.

His silence told me everything. I turned and only made it a few steps before I felt his iron grip encircle my wrist. I had no idea what he would have said, because Theo and Brent entered the room, and Cannon released me. My skin seemed to pulse where his hand grasped me. I didn't want to react to him, but it seemed my body and brain were disconnected.

Theo eyed me, then Cannon. Of course he knew there was tension. Fuck. I think it was so thick in the air, if someone opened their mouth, they would likely choke on it.

"We got everything unlocked." I knew he was talking to me, but he was looking at Cannon. I was going to have to talk to Theo. He was openly challenging

Cannon, and there would only be so many times before Cannon would respond. He would never hurt me. Well, not badly anyway. He wants me too damn much for that.

"Great! Let's go back to my place and see what we find."

We all turned to leave. I looked over my shoulder at Brent, who hadn't moved.

"You coming?" I knew the answer before he shook his head no.

I had no idea what to say to make him feel better, so I just said nothing. He refused to meet my eyes, so I left and shut the door behind me. I knew it wasn't the right thing to do, but there wasn't much else I *could* do.

Chapter Five

When I said, "Let's go back to my place," I guess my crazy ass hadn't recalled that that meant inviting Cannon in my home. There we stood in a standoff at my doorway. Maybe we could meet in the hallway? Oh or go to Theo's. Oh, oh, or we could go back to Cannon's.

"Addison, you could think up hundreds of possibilities. But that's not going to stop me from getting into your-" he trailed off, eyeing my crotch. When his eyes met mine again, my mouth had gone dry and heat had rushed to my cheeks. "Your home."

I looked up at him. I would have sighed, but I didn't think I had enough oxygen in my body to support such an action.

"Cannon, come in." It was a whisper; still he heard it and that was all that mattered. He stepped past me with a wicked smile on his face.

As he passed by, he brushed a hand along my lower belly and murmured, "Oh, I will."

What does one even say to that? *Butt nugget.*

"Is that a book in your pants or are you just happy to see me?"

My hands flew to the back of my shorts and my fingers met the now warm journal. Shit.

"Uh, no…" I neglected to finish the statement and darted to my room. Shoving the book under my pillow, I paused. *Would it be that bad to just read a little bit? I mean, a few pages?* I shook my head and slowly backed away from the book. This was not something I needed to get into, not right then anyway. I walked back out into the living room and closed the door behind me. I also ignored the questioning look Cannon was shooting my way.

"Addison, it looks like a florist shop in here. A particularly morbid one," Theo commented, looking at all of the half-dead bouquets of flowers littering my apartment.

"Yeah if SOMEONE would stop sending them, that would be super great." I eyed Cannon. His eyebrow raised in question and his mouth twisted in a, "what the fuck are you talking about?" expression. He honestly looked confused.

"Addison, do you honestly think I am the flower and candy giving kind of vampire?" When he said it like that, no. He would likely send Russian vodka and condoms. Wait, no, just Vodka.

"Well, if not you, then who?" I asked, looking around at all the piles of flowers I had gotten in the last two weeks. This wasn't even a fraction of the shit that had been delivered over the last few months.

"I'll look into it later," Cannon asserted abruptly.

We all sat on the large couch and Theo opened up the laptop and began typing away at it. I grabbed the tablet and started searching the last applications used and the Internet search history. I said a quick mental prayer that I wouldn't stumble upon his favorite porn sites. Oh dear sweet monkey balls, that would be unfortunate.

There were a number of viewed articles about the rise in gang violence in and around Atlanta. Most of them said the same things. There was a noticeable rise in violent and unsolved crimes in the city. They were such heinous and brutal atrocities that they were thought to be part of a new gang. Most of the victims weren't just drained of blood, but also beaten and savagely attacked. There was no care for gender, race or age. Just as Cannon said, a number of the people killed had been children. I felt bile rise in my throat and splash the back of my mouth. I swallowed it back. I had to get through this.

There were also several articles about some missing persons. A few of these people were affluent, and I wondered why I hadn't heard they were missing. Not that I was really a huge news watcher, but I did follow a few stations on the Internet. The most notable was the son of a congressman. *Shouldn't I have seen something about this on the news?* While I may not keep up with all worldwide events on a daily basis, I did keep up with local events. If this wasn't newsworthy, then nothing was.

I perused his Internet history a bit more. He had been looking up classes to Tang Tu Do. He'd clicked on a few other dojos, even though Darryl's was listed first. Why would he care? Why would he want to take classes? I pushed the questions and the now tightening in my chest down as far as I could. *This isn't helping.*

I looked up to find Cannon studying me. This conversation needed to happen.

I spoke to him mentally.

"Cannon."

"Addison." His mental tone was a throaty purr.

"I need you to stay out of my head. I have to have thoughts that are my own without fear that you're listening in." My mental voice was low and unsure. I hated it because it made me seem weak.

He didn't answer right away. He seemed to be giving this notion of actually doing something kind for someone for no reason genuine thought.

"I can't always turn it off. If you have a mental image or something graphic in your mind, it's as if you stick a picture in my line of sight. I can't help but look. But, I will do my best to give you privacy."

His mental cadence was, well, normal. Nothing sensual or even pissed off. It was just normal and even. It wasn't how he said it, but what he said that took me back. I honestly didn't think he would say yes, so I was speechless.

I felt a cool finger under my chin.

"Close your mouth. You're going to catch flies. Or something else." His eyebrows arched and the corners of his lips twitched upward. I shut my mouth with an audible clack of teeth.

I broke the eye contact and returned to my task. I heard Cannon's laughter echoing off the walls of my mind. Blood rushed to my face because I couldn't help but picture it.

"Well?" I asked no one in particular. Theo had just stepped outside for a mental break. And I of course was stuck in the living room with Cannon. Though he really seemed to be focused on the laptop and his notes.

"Nothing much other than idle notes here and there about possible causes for the increase in violence. Though he seemed to make a link of some high-profile missing persons to the violence." What the hell did that mean?

"Um, what?"

"Okay, the congressman's son, the CEO's twin daughters, and the other three high-profile missing cases."

"You think they were victims?" I interrupted. Cannon then did something I thought above his uptight high-and-mighty ass. The bastard threw his pen at me. Not hard, playfully. I think I was more caught off-guard by his actions than his next words.

"Stop interrupting! No, his guess and mine as well is that these kids are pushers. Possibly even pusher-vampire hybrids. So, no, not victims in one sense."

I knew what he meant. They were possibly victims of being changed, but now, they were possibly the bad guys. The very bad guys. The, "I'll revel in the draining of your blood" kind of bad guy.

This was great information and all, but we needed to find Lachlan. While this information was helpful, there was nothing here that had a neon arrow pointing at it saying, "Here he is!" *It's a damn shame the all-knowing doctor Google didn't know.* I was getting frustrated. If he was in danger, something I thought likely considering the tone of his letter, then I also guessed we had very little time.

One of the other things Brent had done was open up Lachlan's Google account. I had searched through his email and it really didn't have much. It honestly looked like he hadn't used it in ten years. And the asshole had like no spam! *How does that even happen? I get at least three emails a day asking if I want to view hot new singles in my area or if I want to increase my penis size. My penis size is just fine, thanks so much.* There was one thing, however, he did use. Google docs. I opened up a file named "Address book."

At first I didn't see anything I really understood, but after a few entries, I began to recognize the names.

"Cannon, I have Lachlan's address book." I felt pretty proud of the fact that this address book wasn't just any regular kinda little black book. It was for this case. All of the names and entries seemed to correspond with the names in a number of the articles.

"Is it all of his former lovers? Because it would have to be pretty thick for that." I narrowed my eyes at him.

"I'm betting yours would be bigger."

"Oh, it is. I'm a lot bigger." His tone was low and even. I swallowed hard and I tried, I really tried, not to roll my eyes at him. I failed, again.

"No, it's names that I've seen in several of the articles," I said, handing him the tablet.

He took it and eyed the screen. His expression turned from dispassionate to alarmed. Then from alarmed to fury.

"Uh-"

I was cut off by the sudden motion of him flinging the tablet across the room. I had a natural reaction, pulsing my telekinetic ability and stopping the fragile device from smashing into ten thousand shards as it very nearly met the wall. I pulled the iPad back to me, where I released my mental hold.

I wasn't shy about pushing Cannon's buttons, but I also wasn't stupid. I knew he needed to calm down about whatever it was that he saw on that list. Rushing him wouldn't help, even if I wanted to throttle the information out of him. Even if I pictured that very event, over and over.

Theo picked that moment to walk in. And in his amazingly beautiful hand was a familiar box. He was a god among men at that moment. Sexual favors? Fuck yes! I'd do just about anything for what was in that box.

He raised an eyebrow in question. Okay, he tried to, anyway. He was one of those unfortunate people who couldn't raise one eyebrow. So his face looked half surprised and half crazed. His gaze slid to Cannon, who was seething. Shrugging, I got up and eyed that damned box.

We walked into the kitchen. He set the box down and I started some coffee. Sun-up was in a few hours and my energy level was waning.

"Whacha gunna give me for these donuts?"

Without missing a beat, I replied, "A blowjob, drop trow."

Theo guffawed. I couldn't help but giggle.

"That would be like kissing my sister. No thanks!"

Opening the box, he pushed it over. Just like that, my nose was assailed by the scent of the sticky sweet confections. I inhaled deeply. Donuts had this unique scent that I loved, a mix of sweet sugar and a light dough scent. I loved all flavors, but always came back to the original glazed. I picked one up. *Oh, dear, sweet bakery.* They were warm. I shoved half of it in my mouth. The overly sweetness of the glaze almost masked the yeasty dough, but not quite. It was just such a perfect mix.

I hadn't realized my eyes slid shut until I heard Cannon speak, breaking the glaze-induced spell.

"If you're quite done, we have work to do."

I narrowed my eyes at him.

"If you're quite done throwing a temper tantrum, maybe we could get some work done."

I heard Theo suck in a breath of disbelief. Well, I thought it was disbelief anyway.

We both eyed one another for a long moment.

"You know, Addison, I kill people for talking to me like that," he said with an edge to his tone. His words were meant to slice the skin but I was tougher than that.

"You know, Cannon, I just don't give a fuck."

He shook his head and smiled. Not the reaction I thought I'd get.

"You going to tell the class why you had a hissy fit?" I asked, turning to the coffee maker.

"There was a name on that list. A name I specifically told Lachlan not to get involved with. I told him if he had to go to her, he needed to come to me first." My hearing seemed to cut out after the word, *her*. I stopped pouring the coffee into the large mug and turned to face the vampire, who was walking up to the counter.

"Her?" I tried to make the question innocent but it came out an accusation.

"Jealous?" he asked with an amused tone in his voice.

Turning to finish pouring my coffee, I replied, "No just trying to figure all of this out." I knew my tone gave away my lie. In fact, with the envious look I felt on my face, I don't think I could have convinced the Pope I were Catholic even if I were dressed like a nun.

Blessedly, he ignored me and continued, "Lachlan might have gone to see Evgeniya Ogiyevich."

I wasn't even going to attempt to say that name. I would surely butcher it.

"Um, who?"

"A very old witch." I thought for a moment he said vampire, but no, he had said witch.

I blinked at him and tried not to have "that look" plastered all over my face, yet I couldn't help it. Pushers were known for setting up shops as palm readers, witches and fortune tellers. Not that they were wrong for making a buck, but it was wrong to parade themselves around as something they weren't.

"Cannon, there are-" He held a hand up to cut me off.

"She's older than I am." Now, that admission caused

me to pause. Pushers lived a little longer than normal humans but not by much. Cannon was OLD. Like old as dirt.

In the end, I said the only thing I could think of. "Prove it."

He took his pen and wrote an address on the top of the donut box.

"Meet me here tomorrow at 6 p.m." I walked around the counter and stood next to him. I didn't know the address, but it was downtown so it would be easy to get to.

Suddenly, I felt Cannon's arm snake around my waist. Before I had time to make sense of just what he was doing his lips were crushed against mine. This wasn't a kiss that was asking. This was a kiss that was taking and possessing. And damn him back to the ooze he spawned from, but my body softened into it. His hand grabbed the hair at the base of my neck and he tilted my head up. I tried not to open my mouth to him. I really did. His tongue seemed to crash though every barrier. His skin for once felt hot against mine. Super-heated, even.

Just as a delicious throb began to build between my thighs, he let me go. I wasn't panting. Okay, maybe I was panting a little. But, fuck me, he had just taken every wall I had built to keep him out and, with one kiss, demolished them to little more than dust.

Not breaking his nearly black gaze, he called, "Goodbye, Theo. I'll see you tomorrow."

What. The. Hell? Not saying another word, he turned to the door and walked out. All I could do was stand there like a moron with a thumb up my ass.

"Well, chickadee. You're in some deep shit," Theo remarked in a tone that sounded about as shocked as I felt.

"Tell me something I don't know," were the only words my rattled mind could string together. *Deep shit doesn't cover half of what I am into with Cannon. Fuck me up one way and down the other!*

Chapter Six

I could not, for the life of me, focus on my classes at the dojo. I asked Darryl to take my kids in the evening as I really didn't think I would have time for teaching them, then meeting Cannon. Ugh. Cannon. I wished I could say the way he had kissed me wasn't why I was so distracted, but that would be a lie.

His lips felt like slick, heated silk caressing mine. His wicked tongue had — I shook my head to try to clear it and focus, but it was too late. I, for once, hadn't been fast enough. The yellow belt's kick connected with my jaw. Pain exploded and radiated down my neck. I sank to a knee and held up a hand to stop his profuse apologies. My mouth filled with a tangy metallic taste I knew to be blood.

"Addison!" It was Darryl's concerned voice that rang through.

I looked up to find his worried eyes searching mine.

"I'm good." My tongue was swollen from the impact of my teeth having come down on it with his blow. I was slurring my words. I clambered to my feet.

"Clash lie done we pick dish up nes week." I rolled my eyes at the sound of my own words, then walked up to the chairs and sat down to lick my proverbial wounds. I felt a warm trickle of liquid dripping down my chin. *Great, now I'm drooling; this shit just keeps getting better and better.* I raised a hand to wipe it away before anyone saw, and looked down to see it wasn't drool. It was blood. Fantastic.

"Ms. Addison, I'm so sorry!" *Kevin? Kurt? Oh fuck, I don't remember his name.*

I waved him away, saying, "No worriesh. My fal." I smiled and had to stifle a wince. *Damn that hurt.* Darryl, the angel of a man, walked over at that moment and slapped the K-named boy on the shoulder.

"No worries, bud! Addison is a fighter. She's all good," he assured the poor guy.

Darryl led him out.

Stupid, Addison! I pressed the heels of my palms into my eyes until I saw stars. I felt a strong hand grab my shoulder. I didn't flinch as I knew it was Darryl.

"You know the last time you were this distracted?" His tone was so deep it always seemed to rumble against my skin. I knew what he was referring to.

"Yeah, boss. I know." I looked up to find he was

kneeling in front of me. His features were still blurry, as my eyes were trying to adjust.

"Same shit?" he asked.

"Different day," I replied. He knew exactly what I was saying without pushing me. Why couldn't my life be easy? Why couldn't I just work a nine to five and pay my rent on time?

"Come on. Let's clean you up. You look like a human punching bag." And with that, the subject was done. *God bless this man!*

Mother Nature in Atlanta had to be going through menopause. One day it would be in the eighties, and the next in the fifties. Tonight, it was closer to the forties. I was not made for cold weather. Running helped though. I threw on jeans, a long-sleeved shirt, and an overly large hoodie. I couldn't find matching socks, so one cheetah print and one rainbow would have to do.

I opened the door to my apartment only to be greeted with yet another bouquet of flowers. These looked to be a mix made up of star-gazer lilies and baby's breath. It was beautiful, but I was uneasy knowing it wasn't Cannon who was sending them. I didn't have time to think about them, so I shoved them just inside the door. I turned the deadbolt and ran.

Running always seemed to do the one thing I needed to clear my addled head. I had no thoughts of Cannon or Lachlan. No thoughts of flowers or chocolate. The only thoughts I had were the colors of the burnt orange and pink of the setting sun and the rising moon and scents of slightly damp concrete that covered the ground.

The "witch's" house should only take me about ten minutes to get to. I use the term witch loosely, as I didn't believe there was any such creature. It was more likely that she was a pusher preying on innocent people. I would be faster, but I had to slow down a bit due to the fact that I had no idea where she lived.

By the time I got to the place we were meeting, the sky had darkened to a light shade of purple, casting everything in a lavender hue. Though, when I spared a glance down, my skin looked a sickly gray shade. I looked around to survey my surroundings. The house was small and in need of some repair, but it wasn't falling down just yet. She lived just outside of Cabbage Town, and her home kept in with the same esthetic. The houses on either side of the pale-yellow home both had caution tape around them and foreclosed signs littering the overgrown lawns. *Seems like a lovely neighborhood.*

I looked down at my cell phone. It was a few

minutes before 6. It looked like I was the first here. For once, I was early to something! I should be proud. As I was putting my phone into my pocket I felt a sharp stinging sensation on my right ankle.

"Ouch, shit!" I yelled, peering down toward my foot. Standing there rather impishly was a small man. Okay, maybe small wasn't the correct adjective. He was about the size of a rat. In fact, I know the asshole.

"Damnit! Rat, what have I told you about biting me?" I asked as I rubbed the still-stinging spot.

In the next moment, Rat grew to his full height of about four and a half feet, give or take a few inches. Rat was a pusher. He could shrink to the size of a rat, hence his name. And the fact that he looked like his beady-eyed counterpart.

"Addison, haven't seen you in a while." Rat's high-pitched voice was always like an ice pick straight to the brain.

"Haven't wanted to be seen. Where's your brother?" Rat and his twin brother, Twinkie, were never apart. Like EVER. I think they even went to the bathroom together.

Pointing to one of the foreclosed houses, a dirt poof seemed to come off from Rat's brown hair. Rat and his brother were in their thirties, though due to the years of drugs and shit eating, they looked to be in their fifties at least. Even still, the two looked nothing alike, despite the fact that they were twins.

"Hey, Twinkie! It's her, I told you so!" If I had duct tape right, then I would cover his shrill mouth in the silver adhesive. My hands flew to cover my ears.

Out of the house to the left of the "witch's" walked Twinkie. Okay, Twinkie never walked, so much as lumbered. Twinkie stood at about seven foot tall. As if his normal height wasn't tall enough, his pusher ability allowed him to grow to more than twelve feet tall. Rat had always skeeved me out, but Twinkie was a sweetheart.

"Hey, Twinkie," I called to him in a bright tone.

"Hey, Addy!" he called back, waving his giant hand.

I could never get him to call me Addison. But, it didn't bother me like it did with other people.

"What are you guys doing here? Squatting?" I asked, eyeing Rat. Of the two, Rat was the talker. When I first met them, I wanted to call them Pinky and The Brain after the two cartoon mice who always wanted to take over the world. After getting to know them a little, I realized how correct I was. Rat was always scheming something and Twinkie just did what he was told.

"Addison! You wound me!" His hand flew to his

heart and he even stumbled back a few steps. I rolled my eyes at him and sighed. "We do not squat! We are being paid to live here!"

I raised an eyebrow, not believing a single word.

"It's the truth! We are being paid to protect the witch! Tell her, Twink!" He motioned to his brother.

"Yup. It's the truth." Twinkie's low voice seemed to fill the space between us.

"You mean the pusher," I countered.

"No-" Rat started, but the approaching car drowned out his words. It was Cannon. I didn't even need to examine it that closely. I could feel him well before he parked the car and got out. It was a bit like that feeling I get when I know someone is following me.

Rat's eyes went wide at the approaching vampire. For no reason at all, I shivered. Okay, maybe not no reason. But, no reason I wanted to admit to. I felt Cannon's cool finger draw a short line down the back of my exposed neck. I couldn't stifle the shudder that time. I knew he felt the reaction, but refused to acknowledge it any further.

"Cannon, this little tiny guy here is Rat. And, the tall guy is Twinkie." I knew calling Rat tiny would only piss him off. He was just so cute when he was mad.

"Hey!" he said with complete indignation.

"I know who they are." Cannon's words seemed to lick my skin.

"Yeah, Add-i-son! He's our boss. He hired us to watch the witch." I turned to face Cannon. He was far too close, forcing me a step back. Cannon looked down and met my eyes.

"They clearly did a shitty job, as I never received a call telling me my brother came by here." He never took his eyes off of me.

"Mr. Blackwood, he didn't come by!" Rat yelled. His pitch seemed to only get higher. I glanced behind Cannon to make sure his windows weren't shattered. Only by the grace of some benevolent creature they were spared.

"Is there a problem?" It was Theo's voice. I had been so preoccupied with Cannon and the moron twins that I hadn't even noticed he was here.

"Nope! The wonder twins were just leaving," I answered in a rushed tone, completely ignoring Rat. I didn't want to be around Cannon any longer than I had to.

"Wonder twins, ohhhhhhh," Both Rat and Twinkie called. I shook my head.

"Shall we?" Cannon gestured toward the door.

I walked up the stairs and knocked on the door. Nothing happened. I turned to Cannon in question.

His mouth was in a tight white line and his brows were furrowed.

"Now, we wait," he said, turning and walking to the porch swing that looked to be on its last leg.

"We wait?" I asked, looking from Cannon to Theo. *What the hell is this about?*

"Yes. We wait." He sat on the swinging bench.

"Well, okay."

Thirty god-damned minutes later, the door opened. I had never seen Cannon look more annoyed than he did in that moment. That fact actually made me like this "witch" more.

Okay, so when I think of a witch, I have to admit, I picture a haggard, old woman with warts and skin resembling a raisin. Especially since Cannon told me she was older than fucking dirt. That all having been said, what stepped out of the door caused my jaw to nearly hit the floor.

The woman was tall, like runway model tall. Her hair was platinum blonde and hung about to the middle of her back. It was clearly dyed, not that I was judging. Her skin was pale and perfectly smooth. Not a blemish to be seen. *Damn it, but it's eerie. No one is that perfect.* Her face was nothing short of stunning. High ethereal cheekbones, small sloped nose, full Cupid's bow mouth, and delicate chin. Her eyes, though, were a deep brown that seemed tired. What really got me was her body, oh well and her clothing, or lack thereof. She clearly went to the same doctor as Pam Anderson or Dolly Parton. She had her double D, salad-bowl-fake tits shoved into a teeny, tiny white shirt, if we can really call it a shirt, as I could clearly see the pale skin of her underboobs. She had no bra on, and I feared for the safety of her nipples, because if she sneezed, there would be a wardrobe malfunction. *Lord help our eyeballs if that happens.* Her impossibly small waist was bare, and she donned the absolutely shortest pink and green plaid skirt I'd ever seen. That's saying a lot, as I used to work in a god-damned strip club. Her sleek, gazelle-like legs were tipped with what looked to be nude heels identical to the ones Gen had bought for me to wear to Courp Corp. *Just what the hell is this? A joke?*

"Oh my goodness! Cannon! Boo Boo! I'm so sorry, I had no idea you were out here! I'm just so rude!" She sounded like a fucking sprite that was on a sugar high from eating fourteen bags of Skittles and pounding back a few Redbulls. She pranced, there was really no other word for it, over to Cannon. Her underboobs kept popping out as she bounced along. I placed a hand over my mouth as to not say a word. She threw her arms around Cannon in what looked like an awkward hug.

His eyes rolled and I saw a small sigh escape his lips. Looking over to Theo, I had to stifle a laugh. His eyes looked as though they were about to pop right out of his skull. Cannon's eyes flicked to mine. I had to honest to god bite my lip to keep from smiling. *This is like a train wreck. I can't look away, not that I want to! Just what the dick goblin needed.*

"Evgeniya, how are you?" His tone was careful. I raised an eyebrow. I wouldn't go so far to say he was afraid, but cautious. That was something new for the vampire. I felt my joy at the situation falter slightly. *Just what the hell am I dealing with here? A wolf in the skin of a cheerleader?*

"Oh, silly blood sucker! Call me Evie! You know better." I was beginning to like her more and more after that comment.

In my mind I heard Cannon. *"Don't get any ideas."*

Then in my head I heard Evie. *"Oh, oh, I want to play too!"*

My eyes went wide. Having one person in my head other than me was quite enough.

"Okay, so this is fun, but let's all stay out of my head," I said out loud in a not-so-nice tone. I hated feeling like my thoughts weren't my own.

"Meany head. You're no fun," she said, letting go of Cannon and taking a few steps back.

"Could we please go inside, Evgeniya?" Cannon's tone was again guarded.

Evie scoffed at the use of her full name, but walked over to the door. Gesturing for us to enter, she ordered in that same peppy tone, "Come in, pretty please."

For the love of all that is holy. Her whole house was pink and covered with glitter. I'm not talking about a little shine here or there. I'm saying Rainbow Bright and My Little Pony had a love child and named it Barbie. And, she threw up all over this house. I found myself reaching to the top of my head, hoping to find sunglasses resting there. There weren't any. So I did the only thing I could, squinted. It was a little unbelievable. I just knew I was going to come out of this covered in pink feathers and silver glitter.

As if the pink disco ball motif wasn't bad enough, the hallways were lined with shelves. And so beautifully nestled upon those shelves sat dolls. Hundreds of dolls. Not the beautifully made porcelain ones, either. These were the creepy-ass ones that seemed to look right through your soul. To add insult to injury, they all seemed to have some kind of deformity; two heads, a thousand pins sticking through the head, lips sewn shut, burnt to a crisp. Yeah, all the normal stuff.

This chick is not normal! I thought she was a pusher of some kind but I didn't really know anymore. It wasn't as though she had the word "pusher" tattooed on her forehead. I wished I could look at someone and know if they were a pusher or not, but as far as I knew, no one could do that.

I hadn't realized I stopped until Evie spoke.

"Aren't my babies beautiful?" She reached up and plucked a particularly ugly bastard down. This doll's face was half melted and one eye was missing. Small needles were protruding from every part of the figure's body. It reminded me a little bit of a porcupine.

"What are they?" I asked, not able to tear my gaze from the lifeless doll.

"They are my babies. They don't like that you think they're ugly. They have souls, you know. Not every soul is pristine and flawless." She paused and looked at me. Her tired brown eyes sparked with life. "I wonder, Addison, what would your soul look like?" This wasn't just a hypothetical question. She wanted an answer. I looked back to the doll.

I pursed my lips, knowing the answer. Clearing my throat, I spoke, "My soul would be burned and torn apart. It would be far worse than anything I've seen here." My voice came out shaky, but I spoke the only truth I knew.

Nodding, she put the doll back on the shelf, then turned and walked down the hall, continuing through a bead-covered doorway. I couldn't help but wonder if the dolls really did have a soul nestled in each one. I shook my head and walked on.

I pushed the beads aside to see Cannon glaring at me. I rolled my eyes. When was he not glaring, grumbling or otherwise seething? He was sitting on an overly large pink couch that looked as though it had to be made of shag. I sat between Theo and Cannon, as that was the space they left me. I narrowed my eyes at Theo as if to tell him he was a traitor. He shrugged.

Evie sat on a small wooden chair that looked to have been painted white sixty years ago. The paint was crackled and chipped off in a number of places. In fact, there looked to be more decayed wood showing than paint at this point.

"So, Cannon, Boo Boo, who do I need to thank for this long overdue visit?"

Cannon seemed to gnash his teeth and say in a very

controlled tone, "Evgeniya, you know damn well why I'm here."

She stared blankly at him before bringing her perfectly manicured, French-tipped finger to her delicate chin and tapping it in thought.

"Hmmm, you know, I don't think I have any idea. Shnookums, why don't you tell me."

Shnookums? I had to literally bite my lip to keep from grinning. This chick had balls, like the kind that clinked when she walked. My appreciation ratcheted up a notch.

"Lachlan came to see you and I want to know why," Cannon snarled through gritted teeth. Was his face flushed in restraint? *No, vampires don't flush, do they?*

"Oh that yummy brother of yours. I could just lick every inch of him. Don't you agree, Addison?"

I just stared at her, unable to speak. I felt heat rush to my face. *She did not just ask me that?! Traitor! Just when I am starting to like her.*

Before I had time to string two words together into a coherent thought, Cannon began barking at her in what I thought was Russian.

Cannon's tone was heated while Evie's was cool and even. She never took her eyes off of me as she spoke. That seemed to piss Cannon off even more. His Eastern

European accent became thicker the angrier he got. I had to remember to ask him why he and Lachlan had such differing accents.

After an uncountable number of exchanges, they both sat looking at me.

"Umm-" I was cut off by Cannon getting up.

He looked to Theo and snapped, "Come on."

I moved to get up as well, not really knowing what had just happened.

"No, Addison, she wants to talk with you alone."

Feeling a little nervous, I sank back in the pink marshmallow.

Theo and Cannon both eyed me before disappearing through the beads.

Why the hell does she want to talk with me? Much less alone?

We sat in silence for a few heartbeats.

"So…" I trailed off, realizing I had no idea what to say.

"I'm not a pusher. But, you are." Her words had lost a little bit of the peppy hop they had before. She sounded a bit like how I imagined her eyes felt.

"I am. But, for you to know that and communicate with me in my head, you have to be some kind of pusher." My tone was matter of fact. I couldn't help it. The notion that she was a witch was more than insane. Though, after everything I'd seen in this messed up world, it shouldn't have been that big of a stretch. I was just so used to these fake and dishonest pushers preying on people.

"Addison, I'm over one thousand years old. But, that matters nothing now. You don't need to believe me. The question is, why are you here?"

"I want to save Lachlan." I had no idea why I said it like that. Why didn't I say I wanted to simply find him?

She smiled at me. It was the smile a child would get from their mother when they had just revealed who stole the last cookie.

"What if you can't save him? What if what I tell you means that he will be alive but be forever out of your grasp?" Her presence, aura, whatever it's called, changed and suddenly I could sense just how old and powerful she really was.

"I-I don't know," I whispered.

"Addison, you can't save everyone you meet. It will kill you."

"What do I do?" I asked.

"What are you willing to sacrifice for him?" Her question hit me like the force of a physical blow.

"I-"

"And for Cannon? What would you sacrifice for him?"

I had no idea. I bit my lip trying to figure out a way to answer her question truthfully. But she didn't give me the chance.

"You'll have to sacrifice quite a bit." She paused, peering at me. "You can't run forever, Addison. The world will find a way to catch up to you, as will your past."

I'm not sure why this irritated me, but it did.

"Look, I just want to know-"

"How to save him. I know. What if I told you, you could find him but not save him?"

Why couldn't she just be fucking direct?

"I guess I'll have to say that it would be good enough." My feelings were so jumbled and I honestly had no idea how I felt about him. But, I knew I would do anything to make sure he was safe.

She smiled at my words. That must have been the right thing to say because she relaxed into her chair.

"I don't know where he is." Her tone was even. I could hear the truth in her words. I hadn't realized how much hope I held out until I felt it completely evaporate, leaving an emptiness in the pit of my stomach.

"But," she continued, "he was here. Even though Boo Boo out there forbade him from ever coming here."

"Why?" It was a broad question. I had no idea why I wasn't specific, I guess I wanted to see what she would say.

"Boo Boo thinks I'm crazy," she replied in a bubbly tone. She whipped her head to the side and closed her eyes. Is *she listening to something?*

Then she did something that scared the hell out of me. Slowly, she turned her head back to me, eyes flying open. They gleamed like a mirror. I could just make out my own reflection in them. Then she spoke.

"Addy, are you ready to face him? Are you ready to kill him?" Her voice sounded like a thousand voices layered together. It made a chill run up my spine and had me wishing I had an adult diaper on. I would likely piss myself if this shit got any weirder.

"Kill who?" My voice came out in a bare whisper.

"The unkillable ghost. The one from your past."

Then, like a light switch was flipped, she blinked and her eye color changed back to its normal-aged mahogany.

Narrowing her eyes at me, she whispered, "But, I'll tell you a secret: I am crazy."

What. The. Actual. Fuck? This bitch was going to give me whiplash.

"Umm…" was all I could think to say.

"He was looking for a book."

I glared at her. Attempting to have a conversation with this woman was like having a conversation with a parakeet. There was a whole lot of chirping, but not a whole lot of understanding.

"Who was? What?" I was getting exasperated.

"Lachlan, the yummy blood sucker. He was looking for a book. But-" she made a pouty face before continuing, "I didn't have it. But, I told him who did."

"Well? Who had it? What kind of book?" I asked.

She stared at me as though she had no idea what the hell I was saying.

"Who had what, chickadee?"

How could she possibly know that pet name? Only Theo called me that. Then I raised my hand to rub my temples. This had to be what it was like talking to a two-year-old. I took in a deep breath and let it out slowly. I needed to be calm with this crazy person.

"Evie, what was the book Lachlan was looking for and where is it?"

"Oh right, right. The Bessmertnym T'ma." The last two words she used were thick with a Russian or some accent of that sort.

Blinking at her, I raised my eyebrow. I had hoped she would get the not-so-subtle hint, but her stare went completely vacant. I cleared my throat in hopes of something; I'm not too sure what, but something.

"Well, where's the book?" I tried not to sound exasperated, really I did. It didn't work.

She tapped her chin in thought. This went on for an uncomfortable amount of time. Finally, I just couldn't stand it anymore.

"Evie, please, I need to save him." I could hear the desperation in the words, but I didn't care. I did want to save him. Maybe not in all the ways I hoped to, but save him nonetheless.

"Ask the government man," she said nonchalantly as she pulled out a small box from under the table to her right. Opening the lid, she pulled out a tiny neon-pink bottle of nail polish, nail polish remover, and cotton balls.

I had no idea who the government man was but I could tell from her change in demeanor that she wouldn't answer anything more. I stood up and turned to disappear through the beaded entrance.

I was about to ask if she wanted me to ask Cannon to come in, but she shook her head in negation. I just stood there blinking. If she was a pusher, she was the most powerful one I'd ever heard of. Witch or pusher, both scared the shit out of me.

Reaching out to part the beads, I heard Evie's bright voice.

"You'll have to choose one, Addison."

I paused, knowing what she was talking about.

"Right now, neither of them sounds appealing." I pushed past the beads to make my way to the door.

I could hear Evie's shrill laughter behind me and what sounded like hundreds of smaller childlike voices cackling. The tiny voices seemed to surround me, making me feel slightly claustrophobic. My heart was beating nearly out of my chest. I looked up at the dolls. *Are they laughing?* They didn't move. My body was wracked with a shiver. *I need to get the fuck out of this damn house.*

Opening the door, I nearly barreled into Cannon. We would have fallen had he not sidestepped us so that my momentum carried us into a wooden pillar.

I was breathing heavy. Cannon's hard body and strong arms encircling me did something I never thought they could. They comforted and seemed to calm me.

"Want to talk about it?" His cool breath puffed

against my clammy skin, sending a shiver through my body. I shook my head, not really ready to talk about what happened in there.

"I just want to go home." I knew it was the cowardly path to take but I was honestly shaken. If she wasn't a pusher, that meant my paradigm didn't just shift, it was shoved into a rocket launcher and shot to Mars.

"Theo, how about we meet at Addison's in an hour?" Cannon said, stroking my hair. I didn't think about how good his touch felt or how much I didn't want to lose this moment and him to turn back into a raging cock-goblin.

"Come on, let's get to my car and I'll drive you home." His voice was tender. I could only blink at him. I just knew at any moment he would turn in to the ass munch I knew him to be. But, he didn't. Even while we were in the car, he didn't push at all.

Maybe my paradigm exploded and I was in an alternate universe. That had to be it. That was the only explanation. I closed my eyes and sank into the serene silence of the drive.

Chapter Seven

Government man? What the fuck does that mean? And what is the Bessmer T thing?" Theo asked as he brought me a hot cup of tea. I looked up at him adoringly. He gave me one of his dazzling smiles.

"Bessmertnym T'ma," Cannon corrected in a thick accent. Theo and I just blinked at him, still not understanding.

He gave us a look as though he thought we had a combined IQ of six.

"The Immortal Darkness."

"Well that's not an ominous name or anything," I scoffed. I was betting the damn thing had a "666" printed on it.

"It's a book that was written thousands of years ago. It's a bit like a guide to becoming immortal."

I sat up, blinking at him. I glanced over to Theo, who had a bite of donut hanging less than in inch away from his mouth.

"Uh, I'm sorry, what do you mean becoming immortal?" I asked.

"I thought the book was destroyed a few hundred years ago. Anyway, back in Russia there were travelers. Like gypsies. They poured their knowledge into this book. They were desperate to become immortal, but the vampires refused to change them. Dark magic flowed through their veins and at the time, the vampires didn't want to chance changing them. This is where the book came in. From what I understand, there are twenty or thirty ways to achieve immortality. But, only one was successful."

"Evie?" I asked, completely enamored by his insane-sounding story.

"No, she was a fluke. She was born that way. Stopped aging and went insane."

I couldn't meet his eyes. I saw firsthand just what kind of crazy she was, and it scared the hell out of me.

"About two hundred years ago, someone stumbled upon the book again and found the one spell that worked. It took ten master vampires to take the creature down."

"Well, what was it?" Theo asked before I could get the words out.

"I wasn't there, and all but one of the vampires who

were there were killed. The name of the creature and how to kill it is known only by one vampire."

"Who?" Theo and I asked in unison.

"Merriam."

Oh fuck me. *You have got to be kidding me! I can't catch a freaking break.*

We all just sat there in silence. I set my now only warm tea down. It was my favorite, too, with a little dried sage, but now the sweet-smelling liquid only made my stomach turn.

"Isn't she asleep? Or something like that?" Theo asked.

"I heard she woke up a few months ago. She has been looking for her pet," Cannon explained in an amused tone.

"Who or what is that? What, a dog?" I asked, knowing good and well what he would say.

He shook his head, replying, "Close. Lachlan. Her runaway immortal pooch."

Lachlan and his master, consort, whatever. Just his name had a profound effect on me. It seemed to coil around my heart and squeeze until I thought the muscle would burst.

"Okay, I guess we go see her." My voice was hoarse. Even my words sounded stripped and bare, as though they could see my emotions in every syllable.

"I'll set up a meeting. But, it might not be a bad idea to involve the infuriating redhead. What's her name?" Cannon asked, eyeing Theo. I knew damn well he knew her name. He was just being an asshole.

"Gen. In fact, I need to head over there. She gets cranky when her dinner is late. I'll update her and then we will wait on word from you." Theo stood up and walked to the door. I, like the immaculate southern lady I was, got up to see him out. So, maybe I wasn't always a lady, but I could be if I tried.

He turned to face me. Flicking his eyes to Cannon, he asked in a low tone, "You good, chickadee?"

Nodding, I whispered, "I'll be good."

"Love you," he replied, kissing my cheek.

"You too."

I shut the door softly. The audible click of the latch seemed to echo through the apartment. I felt as though we were teenagers who were left alone just after their chaperone left. I didn't want to turn around and admit that I was now alone with Cannon in my home. I could feel the heat wafting off him, even though I knew he hadn't moved from his spot on the couch.

"So, what now?" I asked, not turning around.

"I'm hungry." His tone was guttural and smoky.

Oh shit. I tried and failed to swallow the lump in my throat.

"Okay, um, I have cups of ramen or, well, actually I think that's all I have." I sounded small and distant. Wait, had I just offered him food? *Dumb, Addison, dumb.*

I heard his deep rumbling laughter.

"Come here, Addison. I want to make a deal with you." *Oh this does not sound good.* This was a bad idea, like putting my hand into an active volcano. Not so bright.

I turned and leaned against the door. He looked at me and said nothing. Sighing, I walked over and sat on the couch. I tucked my feet under me grabbing a small white fluffy throw pillow and held the damn thing as if it were a gold brick.

"Okay?" I hedged.

"I want to drink from you when I want. Your blood is…" He drifted off and I saw a shudder wrack his body. It caused my mouth to go dry. "…Sweet."

"O-kay. Um, I don't think-"

He held up a hand, cutting me off. I bit my lower lip, trying to behave. It was god-damned difficult.

"How about, I'll answer one question you have for every feeding. But, I get to choose the location."

"The location?" I asked, my head spinning and my mind filling with a thousand questions.

He moved closer and snatched the pillow out of my grip. *Oh crap buckets. Yeah, like a pillow would really save you from Cannon. Moron.*

"I get to pick where on your lovely body I get to bite you." He reached out and ran a finger down my jaw. Softly, his cool finger traveled south along the sensitive skin along my neck. I swallowed, hard.

"Um, I, okay. I mean, you'll answer any question, truthfully and fully? And for how long with this deal last?" I could feel my heart pounding just in the spot where his finger traced small circles. I had to fight my own reactions to him. Because in that moment, all I wanted to do was close my eyes and see where that wicked finger traveled to.

"I swear I'll answer truthfully." He shifted closer. My heart was now hammering in my chest. I wasn't getting aroused though. *Whatever helps you sleep at night, Addison.*

I waited for him to answer the other question. His brows furrowed as he realized I wasn't going to back down on this point.

"Let's make this a point of time, like three months," he replied. *I could do anything for three months. I mean, couldn't I?*

"Uh, you also, I mean, no getting grabby and trying

to make me have sex with you." I was having a hard as hell time thinking with him this close.

The circles he was tracing stopped. He cupped the side of my face and pulled me closer.

He whispered in my ear, "Addison, I would never do something you weren't asking me to do. But, after my bite, you'll be begging me to fuck you. And I will oblige."

I was breathing rapidly and my head felt like I was swimming. The way he said the word "fuck" made it sound like it was the action in itself. *I am not a pad of butter; no melting, Addison!*

I opened my mouth to add more stipulations or tell him to go fuck himself, but before I had time to check my libido I said, "Okay." *Oh shit.*

I didn't have a moment to protest because he pulled me on his lap. So I sat, straddling him. I had the feeling that I had negotiated poorly. All the while, my sex was throbbing and my body was screaming, *"No, you did great!" Shut up, you whore!*

"Wait, w-what about my question?" My tone was breathless and just a little husky.

I felt his cool breath on my throat only moments before I felt his strangely warm tongue lick a small wet line along my super-heated flesh.

"Ask it," he snarled.

A thousand questions ran through my mind at once. Before I had made up my mind, I heard my voice and felt my lips moving.

"Why are you such an asshole?" *Oh holy hell, I did not just ask that.* Maybe I just thought it really loudly. By the rumbling of laughter I felt under my finger laying atop his chest, I guessed I really had asked. *Great, anger the vampire about to bite you. Wonderful plan, numb nuts.*

"I'm not an asshole, Addison. You just confuse me for human. I'm not human. My humanity died long before I was made into a vampire."

I opened my mouth to ask him what that meant but he shook his head. It was my turn. My turn to hold up my end of this sorted arrangement. What a waste of a question.

He moved a hand to the back of my head, where he fisted it in my hair. He tugged slightly, exposing my throat to him.

"Scoot up." His voice was so deep and thick with its accent, I shuddered. I did as he asked, and sucked in a breath as I felt his distinct hardness pressing deliciously against my core.

He nuzzled my neck a moment before I felt his cool mouth and warm tongue against the silky skin. I could feel my pulse fluttering against his lips. I had to stifle a moan as I felt him suck my skin. It was such a strange sensation, the mix of hot and cold. It very nearly left me breathless.

I couldn't stop the moan from escaping my lips when I felt his fangs slide into my neck. They slid in so easily that it felt as though they always belonged there. I could feel him draw on the wound. Every pull sent a spike of electric pleasure straight to my core, causing my sex to clench.

I felt Cannon's other hand grasp my lower back and pull me toward him. His erection ground into my drenched folds. I couldn't stop my hips from moving, no matter how much I wanted to.

He pulled hard at my neck and thrust up at the same time, causing me to shudder again. I would absolutely come like this, and I wasn't sure I wanted to.

The only sound I could make was a moan, followed by a gasp of breath.

Without warning, he pulled away. For the first time, I felt his absence as a physical loss. *What the fuck is wrong with me?*

He moved his hand from my lower back to my hand, his nearly black eyes holding me in absolute rapture. He moved my hand to cover the wounds from his bite. Then he did something that shocked the hell out of me. He pulled my head down slightly and kissed my forehead. I could only blink at him. He shifted me off of his lap and turned my face to his.

"If I don't stop now, I would devour every inch of you." From his tone, I gathered he was not talking about my blood. He kissed me lightly on the lips and got up, heading for the door. I wasn't sure I could really remember how to speak.

"I'll call you tomorrow, when I hear from Merriam. Rest for now, Addison. You'll need it."

Neither he nor I spoke another word as he stepped through the doorway. I could only stare at the closed door and wonder what the hell has just occurred.

"I'm so fucked," I said aloud to no one. But I didn't know if that fucked was metaphorical or physical. And I wasn't sure I cared. My whore of a libido was winning. Damn her.

Chapter Eight

Sleeping had been easy. Not dreaming, though, had been an act in futility. I had alternating dreams of Cannon and Lachlan. The whole time, I could hear Evie saying that I would have to choose one of them.

I had to work today, but I also wanted to go by the congressman's house. That had to be the government man Evie was talking about. I thought about calling Cannon and telling him, but he would want to come, and I didn't think that was a good idea. His face was just too recognizable. At least that's what I told myself, anyway. The reality was that I really needed some space from him. He was confusing my emotions, and the last thing I needed was to catch any emotions when it came to Cannon Blackwood.

Work was long. Even the cute little kids couldn't lift the fog that seemed to be pressing down around me.

I was, however, surprised to see Erica and her father, Kyle. I thought, after I verbally slapped him in the face, that he'd never come back. I tried, really I had. I went on like six dates with the guy, and never developed any strong emotion toward him other than hating how he chewed his food. I should like him — steady job, cute and the most adorable daughter I had ever seen. Alas, I felt nothing. Today, however, there was something different.

After our confrontation, he was MIA. Now, he couldn't take his eyes off me. I couldn't quite figure it out.

I was almost done with the kids' class. I was ready to get out of there and get to the congressman's house and figure some of this out. I was helping one of the little boys with a better form for his jab when I felt a prickle run up my spine. Turning, I saw what was going on behind me.

Erica was levitating off the mat about three inches. *Oh hell.* I just gaped. My eyes darted around to see if anyone else was looking at her. Thank God, they weren't.

"Class is almost over. I want everyone to do jumping jacks. Then, after ten, it's time for meditation." I turned to look at Erica. Her features were drawn tight, silent tears streaming down her face, and her full cheeks were pink with some emotion I couldn't name.

I walked over to her and pushed her feet to the mat. I glanced at Darryl, who no doubt saw the whole thing and, bless that man, he walked over and escorted us to the back room.

"I'll go talk to Kyle and finish the class." Without another word, he turned and walked out of the small room filled with punching dummies and extra mats.

Erica's soft sobs nearly shattered my heart. I knelt down and put my hands on her cheeks.

"Honey, what's wrong?" My voice was soft and I tried not to burst into tears.

"I-I I-" she took a small breath, "don't know. I just I don't know."

I had assumed she was a pusher. I didn't know for sure, but now I did. I felt the same way when I realized what I was. I remembered the same fear. Frightened that everyone would hate me. But, I quickly realized that everyone hated me not for being a pusher, but for simply being. I shook my head to rid myself of the poisonous thoughts.

"Oh, love." I opened my arms and she nearly knocked me over with the force of her embrace. I simply did what no one did for me. I held her and told her everything would be okay. I told her how beautiful and amazing she was. I told her the truth.

She pulled back and looked at me. Her eyes sparkled with tears and her face looked bleak.

"How do you know it will be okay?!" Her voice was panicked.

"Because I think it turned out okay for me," I said in a soft tone. Her eyes widened. I looked around the small room and saw a small weight ball. I shifted the world slightly and the ball calmly floated to me. I plucked it out of the air. *Thank god it didn't go flying off and hit me in the face.*

Her eyes had officially bugged out of her head.

"You, you, you mean you're a-" She trailed off, looking around, lowering her voice when she said, "pusher?"

I smiled at her and nodded.

"Do people hate you? I just know my dad is going to hate me." Her tone was resigned and defeated. I wondered how long she'd been hiding this, how long she'd felt so utterly alone.

"Oh, honey, your daddy could never hate you."

"But, he hates pushers. He's a member of CAP. He's never going to want to see me." Her shoulders fell and her soft sobs began again. And this time I couldn't blame her. I had no idea Kyle was part of such a hateful group. Citizens Against Pushers, or CAP, were only one of about fifty hate groups. CAP wasn't the worst, but they actively tried to persecute and advocated finding ways to rid the world of pushers. I swallowed hard and prayed Kyle did not disappoint this child. I did not want to have to kill him.

"You're right, I don't know how your dad will react. But, I know he is a good man and loves you." I believed he really was a good person no matter what he said or did to me.

"What now?" she asked, running her arm under her nose.

"Well, I'm not going to make you tell him. But, I'll help explain things to him if you want me to. It's up to you." My tone was even. I needed her to know I would be here no matter what. And, that it was her choice. I wouldn't push her into anything.

Nodding at me, she sighed, "Okay. Let's go tell him."

Such a big, brave girl. When I grow up I want to be just like her.

We left the small storage space to find the dojo had emptied except for Kyle, who was speaking to Darryl.

"Erica, honey, are you okay?" Kyle asked, rushing over to us.

She looked up to me and then met his eyes.

"Daddy. I, I, um…" her words died off, trying to control herself. "I'm a pusher."

I looked at Kyle's face. He looked horrified. Damn him. I wanted to slap him across his fucking face.

His lips pursed into a hard white line before he met my eyes. His features hardened.

"Just what kind of lies and misinformation have you been feeding my daughter?" His rage-filled question shocked me to my core. My mouth just hung open and I blinked at him a few times.

"Um, Kyle. I know this is a shock, but I don't think Addison-" Darryl started, but was interrupted by Kyle's next words.

"Darryl, do you know what kind of whore employee you have working here?" His question was laced with such acid it nearly burned my exposed skin.

Stifling a wince, I held up my hand to stop Darryl from killing the asshole.

"Look, I'm sorry about what happened between us. But this isn't about me or you. This is about a scared little girl who is absolutely terrified that her daddy won't love her anymore. Look at her, Kyle."

He did. Erica was tucked so close to my side I could feel her trembling.

"You're welcome to call me names when she's not around. You're welcome to hate me. But, right now, your daughter needs to know you still love her." His face seemed to soften at my words.

He took a few steps closer to Erica. She cuddled closer to me out of what I assumed was fear. That seemed to make something click in Kyle. His shoulders relaxed and the corners of his mouth lifted in a small smile.

"Erica, why do you think you're a pusher?"

"Because, I can, um, well, float. And, Daddy, Ms. Addison had nothing to do with it. It's been going on for months." His eyes widened then fell. He looked defeated.

"You saw her, I assume?" I knew he was speaking to me even, if he didn't meet my eyes.

"Yes, Kyle. Listen, I know there are a lot of people who hate pushers, but it's really not that bad," I tried to explain.

"Not that bad? How would you know?" He stood up, meeting my eyes. His face was flushed and his own eyes were rimmed with red.

"Because I am one." I bent the world slightly once more and locked on to Erica's bag. The bag, however, was lighter than I thought, so it went flying toward me and caused me to step back a few paces to not knock my own head off. I walked back to Erica and handed the bag to her.

"I know this is a shock, but I'll be here to help," I tried to reassure them.

He looked dejected.

"Daddy, do you hate me?" She asked the question as though she knew he would say yes.

He met her eyes and knelt down. "Erica, I'll always love you. No matter what. Don't ever doubt that." She ran head long into his arms.

After a few moments, Kyle whispered, "How about you go to Mr. Darryl. I bet he has a bag of Skittles for you."

She nodded softly. Before turning, she looked at me and gave me a sweet smile. I smiled back.

Standing up, Kyle's eyes met mine. "Addison, I-"

I held up a hand, cutting him off. "This isn't about you or me right now. So, if you have more poison you want to throw my way, do it on a different day." Okay, yes, that may not have been fair, but damnit, I was not up for more verbal bashings.

"No, Addison. I'm sorry. What I said back there wasn't fair. I-I don't know what to think or how to feel and I took it out on you."

"I'm sorry, too." My voice was soft. I *was* sorry. I hadn't wanted to hurt him.

"I just hated them, I mean you. No, wait that's not what I mean. Shit." His hand went to the back of his neck and he began rubbing it.

"You hated pushers, what I am. And now your world has just imploded?"

"Pretty much," he replied with a little chuckle in his voice.

"Look, take your daughter home and love her. That's all you need to do. She will gain better control of her ability as she grows."

He nodded, looking at his daughter, who was walking back with a bag of Skittles. He gathered her stuff and picked her up, hugging her fiercely. He turned to face me and mouthed, "Thank you."

I nodded and they left.

Darryl walked over to me, threw an arm around my shoulder and squeezed.

"So, I'm glad I didn't have to slap the shit out of him," Darryl said matter-of-factly.

"Darryl!" I chided.

"Hey, no one treats my Addison like she's nothing. And no one calls you a whore and deserves to see the light of day. I don't have kids, but if I did, I'd want you."

I tried hard to swallow, but every single emotion I had in my body seemed to hit me at that exact moment. And, damnit, tears pricked my eyes. But, like always, I refused to let them spill.

"Well, if I had a dad, I'd pick you," I croaked.

He cleared his throat and grumbled, "Get out of here before we start singing Kumbaya or some shit."

I laughed and went to get my stuff.

Leaving, I called over my shoulder, "I love you, you grumpy bastard."

"I love you too, short stuff."

I left knowing I was beyond lucky to have him. Had I have been a little girl again, I knew I would have had someone would loved and wanted me. Just that knowledge alone seemed to act like a salve on part of my broken soul.

Chapter Nine

No one in their right mind is going to believe you're a private investigator dressed like you just stepped foot out of the gym." Theo's tone was amused.

"So, what's your plan?" I asked, fingering the drawstring on my gym pants.

"Um, let me think about it." He rubbed his chin in mock thought. Raising his finger up as though an idea had hit him, he finished, "Wait for Cannon." His lips turned up in a half smile.

Narrowing my eyes at him, I shook my head.

"He's too recognizable. There is no way Congressman Tennit would even open the door with Cannon standing there and you know it."

"This is a bad idea, Addison."

Yeah, no kidding.

"How about we just toss out the plan and knock on his door."

I glanced outside the car window. The sun had set

long ago and the dark sky lent a soft blue glow on the ostentatious white house. The building was huge. Though the top two floors were dark, the bottom floor windows had amber light spilling out of them. The yard was impeccably maintained.

The light sprinkling of rain had now turned into fat drops pinging against the car roof. I didn't want to do this in the rain, as it tended to limit my speed and I had no idea what we would be getting into.

Theo sighed.

"This is dumb."

He was right. Of course he was. But his tone led me to believe that he would be joining me in my stupidity.

"Hey, I haven't gotten us killed yet, have I?" I asked shyly.

"Oh God, chickadee, the confidence you have just instilled in me is threatening to overwhelm me." He swiped a hand across his forehead as though there were a buildup of sweat there. It made his already dark skin seem yet darker.

"Shut it," I scoffed, slapping his hand.

We got out of the car. Walking to the house, we didn't run as one might expect, given the rain and the fact that Theo didn't have a damn umbrella. We didn't want to miss what little we could see of our surroundings. We really had no idea what we would be walking into. With every step closer to the door, I had a sinking feeling that this wasn't just a bad plan, but a really bad plan. I pushed the negative feelings and thoughts back and continued to walk toward the door.

I rang the bell and tried like hell to brush off all the water I could. It didn't work. I was close to resembling a wet dog. I just prayed I didn't smell like one. I heard rustling behind the door, then a soft click of the latch, and a woman peered out from the crack of the door.

"Can I help you?" the woman asked. I couldn't tell much from the small crack other than that she had salt-and-pepper hair, she was taller than me, but not by much, and her light-brown eyes looked tired and worn.

"Maybe, um, I heard Adam was missing. I mean, from what I've read in the paper"-" She sucked in a breath and slammed the door.

Fuck! I had to get her to talk to me. I didn't have time to think before I heard the words coming out of my mouth, "Wait! Please! My boyfriend, he's missing. I-I just want to find him!" Why had I said that? And why had it sounded so painful and real?

The door cracked again. The woman's eyes that look so tired were rimmed with red.

"Why come here?" Her voice was hoarse.

"I-I don't know. All I know was that Adam's disappearance sounded a lot like my boyfriend's. I'm not trying to do anything other than find him." Meeting her eyes, I begged, "Please." What had started out as just attempting to pump these people for information had turned into something far more real than I had expected.

"Ma'am, we just want to find him and didn't know where else to go. The police have no answers and because they aren't married and we're not family, they refused to tell us a whole lot." Theo's voice was soft and caring.

She sighed and stepped out on the porch. I cocked my head at her. Most people would invite us in, but whatever.

"I don't want to disturb my husband. He's working." Her voice had a slight southern twang, much like my own, except hers was thicker. In fact, she sounded embarrassed she didn't invite us in.

"I'm Addison and this," I motioned to Theo, "is Theo."

"I'm Beverly, Adam's mother."

"Mrs. Tennit. I have no idea if Lachlan and Adam knew-" Her eyes went wide at the mention of his name. My eyes shot up in response.

"Did you know Lachlan? He's in his thirties." Yeah right. "Tattoos, blue eyes, Shaggy light-brown hair…" I trailed off, not needing to ask her any more questions. Her face fell even further and she wouldn't meet my eyes. Her shoulder slumped, telling me she knew exactly who I was talking about.

"He came here asking about Adam. He spoke with my husband. He asked all kinds of questions about Adam being a-" she lowered her voice, whispering, "pusher."

"When was this?" I asked, willing my pounding heart to calm slightly.

"About two or three weeks ago. My husband kicked him out after he asked about him being a, well, you know." She sounded so disgusted.

It was hard not to get pissed off or angry with people like that. Misguided people who feared everything they weren't.

"Adam was a pusher, wasn't he?" I didn't need to ask the question. It was written in her prejudice.

She could only nod.

"Bev!" I heard a distant male voice call from behind her. Her eyes went wide in alarm.

"Look, I gave your boyfriend two addresses. A warehouse Adam owned for a business he was starting up and his apartment. I'll do the same for you. But you have to go." She rattled off the two addresses and Theo jotted them down in his phone.

She opened the door and slipped inside. I heard the male voice begin yelling at her, demanding to know who was at the door.

"Ma'am, we will be here any time you would like to talk about Jesus Christ and all he has to offer your soul," Theo called to the closed door.

The shouting stopped and we walked back to the car. I turned back to glance at the door. I wanted to go back to be sure he didn't hurt her. I started to when I felt Theo's hand grab my arm.

Shaking his head, he commented softly, "It would only make things worse." He was right. Of course he was. And I hated it.

We got into the car and both sat there for a moment.

"I would ask what now, but I think I know." Theo's tone was resigned.

"On James!" I joked.

He rolled his eyes and started the car.

The first place we tried was the apartment. We found a bunch of nothing there. In fact, take the dump Brent lived in and multiply it by about thirty, and that was the mold-covered garbage can he called a home. It seemed like no one had lived there for months. We moved on quickly, marking that place down as a loss. Just before leaving, I paused. Had Lachlan come here and done just what we had? Were we just following in his footsteps? It made me wonder when we would make that fatal mistake. The one that got him caught. I pushed the thoughts aside and walked to the car. I hoped we'd find something, anything, at the other address.

Standing outside of the large flat building, I flinched as lightning struck behind it, illuminating it from behind.

"A big-ass, dark warehouse, on a rainy night. Didn't Wes Craven direct this movie not long ago?" I had to nearly yell at Theo. The rain was pouring and we were well passed drenched.

"Addison, I want you to remember this was your stupid-ass idea. Not mine."

I nodded as we crept behind the long, flat building.

The warehouse was located in a pretty nasty area in downtown Atlanta. So, of course, I knew right where it was. Along the rear of the building there was a line of dense trees. That made me more than a little nervous. I had no idea how deep the trees went, but I swore it felt like there were eyes peering at us. It was fucking unnerving.

We'd circled the building once, looking for cameras or any kind of way in. There was a padlocked door at the back and no cameras that we could see. *This is not a stupid idea, really. Yeah, whatever helps you sleep at night, Addison.*

Theo tentatively reached for the door handle. I heard a light click, then the door slid open a fraction of an inch.

Theo looked from the door then back to me, his eyes narrowed.

"Oh, because this is a wonderful sign," he whispered.

I shrugged and motioned for him to open the damn door. I mouthed, "Like a damn Band-Aid."

"What? I can't read lips," he hissed in a frustrated tone.

"For fuck's sake, open the door!" I hissed right back.

Rolling his eyes, he pushed the door open.

When it rains everything here in the south tends to take on a slightly fish smell. It's not a wonderful scent, but it's also not horribly displeasing. But, when that door opened, I was hit with an odor unlike anything I had ever smelled before. I had to imagine the scent that was permeating from that building could only be described as something dead. Something really big and dead. Lots of somethings.

Theo and I turned around and, fuck it, stealth be damned. I couldn't hold back. I vomited right there, praying I wasn't splashing anything on my shoes. Once my stomach had completely emptied on the pavement, I tried to stand, but my abdominal muscles cramped and I thought staying hunched over for the moment might be a fantastic idea. I felt a warm hand on my lower back followed by Theo's reassuring voice.

"Chickadee, you okay?"

All I could do was nod as I slowly stood up. *What the flying hell is that horrific smell?*

"Addison, we need to call Cannon." His tone was even and firm.

"Why?" I rasped. My mouth tasted like what I imagined battery acid tasted like and, well, I won't even venture a guess to its smell. My throat felt raw and burned.

"Addison, there is something dead in there-" he paused, swallowing, clearly he was gathering himself, "and from how bad that is, I'm guessing it's either massive in size or number."

I sighed, knowing he was right. I dug around in my pocket and retrieved my phone, walking toward the tree line in hopes the rain coming down in waves would ebb slightly, given the branches. I dialed Cannon.

"Where the fuck are you?!" Cannon bellowed into the speaker.

"Hello to you too, sunshine," I cooed.

"Addison! Where are you?" His tone quieted but still held its edge.

"Um. Can't you tell through our bond?"

"It's not a fucking GPS locator. Do I need to pull you? Or-"

Fuck me, I did not want to get pulled. I explained where I was and why. There was a prolonged silence.

"Hello?" I questioned, pulling the phone from my ear to be sure the call was still connected. It was.

"I'm trying to decide the best way to kill you," he snarled.

I tried not to scoff into the phone. Really, I tried. I failed.

"Cannon, we're fine! We just may be in over our-" My words were cut off by a strangled sound behind me. I whirled to find Theo's head bend to the side and some vampire feeding from him. I could only see the top of this monster's head. Short, brown hair that was drenched. Theo's body was limp and pale. The look on his sagging face caused everything to freeze. I dropped the phone.

The world stopped. The scent of wet earth died, the

sounds of a chattering phone and rainfall fell away. Everything was replaced by paralyzing fear and the sound of my own heartbeat thundering just behind my ears. I ran headlong toward them. I didn't give two shits about myself. But, I had talked Theo into this and I had to get us out of it. If not us than him.

The vampire threw Theo away like a used napkin he was done with. He smiled at me, blood dripping down his mouth and chin. His snakelike tongue darted out in search of the fading ruby droplets. The rain was slowly washing away the red streaks. This vampire had to be just south of six feet tall. He was about the same pale complexion as Gen, but his eyes. His eyes were all black. No white left to them.

I ran as fast I could, hoping to get to Theo and try to get him out of there. I had to get to him. Maybe it was the rain or mud, but the beast caught me before I even had time to register what was going on. He slammed me in to the wall directly behind me. My head hit the brick exterior so hard I briefly saw stars. White-hot pain exploded behind my eyes and caused me to let out a shrill, pain-filled scream. *How the fuck did he do that? I'm hella fast, even when the conditions aren't the best. This ass nearly plucked me out of super speed like it was nothing.*

The vampire crushed his hand around my throat, making it feel as though I were breathing through a straw. He leaned in and licked the side of my neck. I tried punching him and kicking him but the mother-fucker didn't budge.

"I know you." His voice seemed to slither around me. "He told us he wanted you alive. But, he didn't say you were so sweet tasting."

"Wh-" I tried to get the question out but he only tightened his already iron grip on my neck. I began pulling on his arms, digging my nails into his flesh. He didn't even flinch.

"I think I just want a taste."

He briefly released my throat enough for me to suck in a breath and say one word.

"Adam?" It was a rasp that was barely audible, but with just that sound his features hardened. He bared his teeth in a snarl and his eyes bored into mine.

"Hey, honey, did you miss me?" a wonderfully beautiful voice rang from behind the vampire. I didn't need to see her. I knew by her tone who it was.

Gen, bless the crazy bitch, was there. Adam stiffened and released his hold on my throat, sending me to my knees, gasping to fill my lungs. He whirled to face Gen.

I glanced up to see her standing there, like a beacon of hope twirling a sword in her hand. I could tell just by the way she flipped and caught the damn thing that she knew how to handle it. My vision had returned to somewhat normal and I saw Adam had backed up until he was just a few steps to my right. I glanced up at Gen and then down to Theo's unmoving form. I didn't hesitate. I rushed Adam, punching the only thing I could reach. His nuts. He went ballistic with rage, but not with pain. There was no screaming or hollering. It was like the fucker couldn't feel pain. I still had no idea what his pusher ability was, but surmised that not feeling pain was part of it. Cannon was right about these pushers turned vampires, they were out of this world insane.

I glanced to Gen, who shifted from one foot to the next in clear anticipation of the fight to come. The saying, "Don't bring a knife to a gun fight," came to mind and seemed to be rather appropriate. Don't bring a pusher to a vampire fight. I was out classed and out gunned. But that didn't mean I had to be a helpless victim. I managed to scramble to my feet. I had to let Gen handle this. I would only be in the way. I had to get to Theo.

Gen charged. I used my speed to dodge the impact.

I tried to run at full speed, but it only caused me to slip to my knees, thus making me roll over to Theo. I fought my fear and frantic heart rate to get to him. His body looked lifeless and pale. And pale for a black man, yeah, that just wasn't a good thing. I reached for his neck, hoping to feel a steady thump. I felt nothing.

No, please, please, please. I felt tears prick my eyes. I moved to the other side of his neck to see if maybe I wasn't doing this right. *I have no idea what I was doing.* His skin was slick from the persistent rain. Or at least that's what I was telling myself. I let my fingers rest against his neck. I felt a faint thump against my skin and sobbed with relief. A faint heartbeat I could do something with. But dead was not an option.

I glanced down at his ravaged neck. The skin gaped as though he hadn't just been bitten, but gnawed on. The wound oozed a slow trickle of blood. I did the only thing I could think of, I took my soaking shirt off, rung it out, and pressed it against him firmly.

I turned my head to view Gen and Adam. They were fast. Not nearly as fast as I was, but still impressive. He was managing to somehow dodge her sword. Then he made a mistake and she slashed up and managed to cut his left hand clean off. He didn't even stumble. The fighting paused as he held the gushing limb up.

He looked at Gen and smiled. It was a cocky, knowing smile. *What the fuck does he have to smile about? He just had his hand cu-*

He yelled out and strained slightly and the goddamn limb grew back in an instant. Oh shit.

"Gen! He's a regenerator! He's not going to feel any pain. You need to get his head!" I yelled.

"I fucking see that, captain obvious!" Gen snarled back.

I looked back down to Theo. I wanted to help Gen, but couldn't without leaving Theo. *Fuck. Wait, maybe I can.* I moved my attention to Adam.

I had never tried to do something like this before, and hoped I could at least slow him down. I focused on his newly grown hand, slowly letting my power coil around it. I had to shift the world around it. Nothing happened. I focused harder. Still nothing. I closed my eyes. I pictured how I wanted to twist his arm behind his back. I let the image settle and then opened my eyes. He'd shifted slightly, but I again mentally grabbed his arm and pulsed my power. His arm flew behind his back.

While this was a great idea in theory, in practice it might have been, well, hasty. All of Adam's attention had thoroughly turned to me. I could do nothing but hold his arm behind his back. All of my mental ability was at its limit and I couldn't stop the train that was now coming at me. Gen didn't have time to stop him. I didn't have the strength or ability to do anything other than hold his fighting hand in place and press down on Theo's neck. I tensed just before he crashed down on top of me.

He hit me once. Pain exploded along my right eye, through to the back of my head and down my neck. I thought the pain would flow throughout all of my body. The world tilted, went blurry. I had to protect Theo. As the world slowly faded, I hunched over Theo, hoping my body would shield him from any more pain. Pain I had caused.

Just before the blackness overtook me, I thought I saw Adam's head rolling passed my limited sight. But I chalked it up to wishful thinking. I fell headlong into unconsciousness.

Chapter Ten

I snuggled deeper into the softest cloud I had ever slept in. It had to have been made out of warmed silk, fuzzy warm blankets, and tons of feathers. I just knew clouds felt like this. I felt a smooth cool body wrapped protectively around me. I hadn't remembered sleeping with someone. But, it was too comfortable and nice to even think about moving.

Then the pain hit me. White-hot pain exploded and I sat up, gasping for breath.

I blinked rapidly, hoping to understand where I was. I was in a room that was stark white. Even though there was no light spilling in from anywhere, the room's bright-white decor was enough to feel like my head was slowly being compressed in a vise. There was this annoying buzzing in my ear that I couldn't quite get rid of.

Oh shit! Theo! I flew out of the bed, tripped on some fuzzy rug, and bolted to the door. Just as my fingers grazed the doorknob I felt strong arms circle around my waist.

"Addison!" The buzzing sound had focused a bit more.

I fought the hold the person had on me. In my stiff befuddled mind, I assumed it was Adam.

"Damnit, Addison, stop!"

I paused, trying to understand. My skin grew cold with the cool air and the man behind me.

"Addison, it's Cannon. You need to calm down." His voice finally solidified into its normal cadence. He sounded as though he were attempting to coax a frightened deer.

"Where am I?" My voice was rough. It hurt to talk. A shiver ran up my spine and goose flesh covered my body. I felt my body shift in Cannon's arms as he lifted me up. He was taking me back to the marshmallow of a bed. It was about that moment I realized I was completely nude. I met Cannon's eyes and the corners of his mouth twitched up into a sly smile. I rolled my eyes.

"You're in my bedroom. Or, rather, in my bed." He raised an eyebrow at that last statement and his tone had a hint of amusement in it. Normally I loved to banter with Cannon, but while I wanted to know why I was naked I wanted to know about Theo more.

"Where's-" I rasped. I swallowed, hoping that would help clear my dry throat. "Where's Theo?"

His expression fell, the smile turning into a pained expression. His eyes for once wouldn't meet mine. *No, no, no.* My heart stopped.

"Addison." His voice was calm and low. "When I got there Gen was frantic and thought both of you were dead. I took you both back here. But, Theo had lost a lot of blood. I did everything I could. But, Addison…" He drifted off, clearly he was choosing his words carefully.

I felt warm tears trail down my cheeks. My eyes burned with the overwhelming emotion and pain I was feeling. I had done this.

"Addison, I had to give him my blood. He may wake up a human or a vampire, or not at all. That depends on his willingness."

The tears had at some point turned to acid and burned my skin. I whipped the wetness away.

"What does that mean?" I was confused.

"Changing a human isn't easy. There is a blood exchange that needs to take place, the bond needs to be strong, and there needs to be a willingness. Sometimes, okay, a lot of times, it doesn't work. My blood is strong and he's bound to Lachlan, so that helps. But he was so close to death that I couldn't drink from him. I could only get a few drops."

"I don't understand, Cannon!" I cried.

"Addison. Listen. I gave him my blood in hopes that it would heal him. Our blood can do that. But, he was so close to death that I'm not sure it will work. He could recover and be fine." My heart was hammering at the thought. He must have seen the hope enter into my face because he continued, "But if he dies, he could possibly rise again, or he might just stay dead. Addison, I don't know which way it will go. It depends on him at this point."

"Where is he? I want to see him," I asked. My head was spinning, not just because of all of this information, but because it was literally spinning.

"Addison, I swear I'll take you to see him, but you were knocked out cold. You need to relax. I gave you some of my blood as well. That's why-"

"You did what?!" I snapped. "Oh my God. Am I going to-"

"No. Addison, you're not going to turn."

"I want to see Theo. Now." I was firm in this. He must have seen it in my face, because he sighed and stood up. His pale, sculpted body did not in any way go unnoticed.

He was cut, yet somewhat lean. Every movement and twist of his body caused a delicious ripple and contraction of his muscles. His chest was broad, but not obscenely so; it lead into a taut, tapered waist. He, his, um, manhood? Coc- no way, so not thinking that word. But, oh my hot damn he was uh, well-endowed. He turned to walk into the closet, and his ass. Okay, I'll just say he had an ass that would make a person get down on their knees and thank whatever benevolent god created such a being. Oh the things I would–

I heard a low chuckle from the closet. I groaned. Clearly I was telegraphing. But, none of that mattered. I had to get to Theo.

"Hey, where are my clothes and why am I naked?" I yelled.

"I burned your clothes. They were filthy," he commented nonchalantly, walking out of the closet. He had suit pants on and they hugged him low on his hips. *Oh to be a pair of his pants in the next life.* He raised an eyebrow at me in what looked like question and amusement.

"Get out of my head!" I growled.

"I can't help it when you send images that I like." His tone was husky. I swallowed, trying to ignore the tingle that tone sent right to my core.

"Well, what am I supposed to wear?" I asked somewhat hoarsely.

He held up a stack of clothing and tossed them to

me. I quickly rifled through them. A drawstring pair of sweat pants, and white button-down shirt that read *Armani* on the tag. I nearly choked.

"This shirt is worth more than I make in a damn month! Don't you have a T-shirt?" I asked.

"No, Addison, I don't. I guess you will just have to deal with it." He crossed his arms and leaned against the doorframe as though he had been waiting on me for hours. I rolled my eyes, not even asking for privacy. I knew Cannon. He would give me privacy just after he pulled a tiger wearing a two-piece bikini, and juggling all of the members of *NSYNC, out of his ass.

I stood up and realized just how badly I needed to go to the bathroom.

"Um," I started, but Cannon the fucking mind reader just pointed in the direction of the bathroom. I darted in, clutching the clothes to my chest.

After I took care of everything I could, considering my toothbrush and such weren't there, I went to slip on the clothes.

Oh this is a problem. The pants were way too big. There was about a foot left dragging and massive gaps in the waist. I kicked them off and slipped the shirt on. It nearly reached my knees. I buttoned it up and stepped out of the bathroom.

Cannon's eye shot up and his mouth flattened into a hard white line.

"Pants. Now," he snarled.

"Cannon. They are way too big! There's no way I can wear them. I'll be tripping over myself," I replied, trying not to roll my eyes.

He grumbled something that sounded like fine, but I couldn't be sure. He led the way and I followed behind him, rolling up the sleeves of my new dress.

I don't think I had ever hated myself more than I did in that moment, standing next to Theo. I've hated myself for the mistakes I made in my past, for a long time. I thought I was fixing myself and my impulse control issues. *But, here I am back to the same thoughtless person I used to be. Hating myself is easy; liking who I am takes a lot more effort.*

Theo lay unmoving in a bed. Not like a hospital bed, but a lush, white one. There were a number of monitors beeping and an IV line connected to him.

I couldn't will my legs to move. I didn't want to breathe for fear that somehow that would only cause him more pain. I felt a large hand rest on my lower back. I glanced back to Cannon. His expression was completely unreadable, but his intention was clear as he put pressure on my back, pushing me forward.

I took one step and heard the latch on the door click. I turned to see Gen. Her face was pale. Her lips were set in a tight white line and her eyes were narrowed.

In a low tone she hissed, "You have a lot of nerve being here."

What could I say? She was right. I shouldn't be here. *Why am I here?* I think a part of it was I was looking for absolution. For Theo to magically wake up and be okay again.

"Step out, both of you," Cannon muttered in a low, controlled tone.

Gen turned and stalked out and I followed close behind her.

I shut the door behind me and crossed my arms in front of me, readying for her attack. The attack I knew was coming. The attack I deserved.

"Addison. Theo loves you more than just about anything. He would die for you and he still very well may. But all you do is use. You only use him for what he can do for you." She began to pace the small hallway.

I could say nothing. It was all true. I was a user, and I would likely always be.

I just stood there, hoping to understand how everything went so damned wrong.

"The worst part about all of this is that I can't blame you," she whispered.

My head flew up and I met her pained gaze.

"Um. What?" I managed to get out.

"You made a stupid decision. But, Theo called me and I was there the whole time. I was too damn distracted listening to you and Cannon to notice that fucking vampire had him." She choked on the word *vampire.*

"Gen, you're wrong. You being there or not, it's still my fault." My throat felt raw and the words pained me.

"No. I'm mad at you, don't get me wrong. But I didn't try to stop it."

"Let's just go see him." I sighed, not really knowing what to say to make any of this better.

We both entered the room to find Cannon leaning over Theo, whose eyes were open.

"Theo?" I croaked, hurrying over to him.

He turned his head to face me. I expected him to hate me or look at me with distain. Instead, his gaze was only filled with love.

"Oh my God, Theo, I'm so sorry. I don't-" I was stopped by Cannon's pointed look and Theo, who tried to speak but couldn't seem to force the words out.

"He looks like he's going to be fine. Okay, as fine

as one can be without fangs. We need to let him rest."
Cannon was right.

I walked over and kissed Theo's cheek and whispered,
"I love you. And I'm so sorry." It just seemed so trite, but
there was nothing else I could say. I left the room in a hurry so no one could see the tears spilling down my cheeks.

"Addison!" Cannon's voice boomed behind me just
as I got to the frosted glass door. I paused.

"Listen, I need to go for a run," I mumbled, reaching for the doorknob. I really needed to just run. To get
away. And I really didn't care what he said.

"There's a difference between running and running away." His words slithered around me, causing
me to halt any forward movement.

"What the hell is that supposed to mean?" I whispered, not facing him. I knew exactly what he was saying, but my pride would have none of it.

"Addison, it's your MO. Things get rough and you
run." He was right, though I sure as hell wasn't about
to tell him that.

"I always come back. Isn't that what matters?" I
asked, turning to face him finally. Oh crap. He was
much closer than I expected. I took an instinctive step
back and felt the cold glass penetrate the thin material of Cannon's shirt.

"No," he purred, taking a step forward. "That's not what matters. It's how you handle the situation in the moment that matters." I hated him because he was still right. He must have seen it in my face, because he reached up and laid his palm against my cheek. Fuck me. It was comforting. So comforting that I really didn't want to admit it. My head wanted to rebel against what my body was feeling.

"How were you changed?" I had no idea why I blurted that question.

He withdrew his hand from my face. His face hardened from the foreign soft, almost caring features to its normal unreadable stone.

Turning, he growled, "Go for your run."

"Now who's the one running away?" It was a stupid thing to say. I knew it the moment the words fell from my lips.

He turned slowly and walked to me. He pushed me back against the wall with his body. That same hand. The one that had so sweetly caressed my cheek, reached up and wrapped around my throat. He applied just enough pressure to be uncomfortable. I was still able to breathe. He shifted my head to the side and I felt his cool breath tickle the hairs just under my ear. It lit my skin on fire and covered it in ice all at the same time. My heart beat wildly in my chest.

"There's no going back, Addison. Once you hear this story. There's no going back to how things used to be." His voice was guttural and rough. *It doesn't turn me on at all. Really. I swear.*

"What do you mean?" I rasped.

"You may think I'm a monster now. But, this knowledge will only confirm that. Are you ready for it, Addison? Are you ready to know the beast?" His grasp around my neck tightened. I felt his tongue lick a lazy line from my collarbone up to my jaw. A shiver wracked my body.

Was I ready? It didn't really matter if I was or not because I heard the word I found myself always saying to this man.

"Yes."

Chapter Eleven

I sat on Cannon's bed, hugging a pillow against my chest so tightly that I thought it might explode into a thousand feathers.

Cannon leaned against the door, his arms crossed over his broad chest. We'd been sitting like this for at least twenty minutes. I couldn't relax. I just knew when I did he would hit me with a bomb. He didn't relax either. He stood there motionless, not breathing. It was unnerving. Nevertheless, this had to be his choice to tell me. I couldn't push him or force him into it. No matter if I wanted to or not.

"I was turned about twenty years before Lachlan. Though, that's not what I told him. I was older than when I turned him. Our mother had me early in life and she had Lachlan late." I was trying to do the math in my head. She had to have been really young.

"She was fourteen. That wasn't too surprising in those days. But she was in her early forties when she had Lachlan and that was unheard of." His voice softened somewhat when he talked about his mother. "What has Lachlan told you?"

I thought back to how Lachlan was changed.

"Well, he said your father left before you were born. Then you left. That's really all I know."

"I was eleven when I left my mother's home. My mother hated me. Not for any other reason than what my father did to her."

"What did he do?" I clutched the pillow tighter as if it would cushion the blow I knew was coming.

"He raped her." Three words. That's all it took for my heart to break, not just for her, but for Cannon.

"I don't blame her for hating me. I reminded her of the man who ripped her innocence from her. He left her broken and with child. Her family, all except her grandmother, abandoned her. Then I came, looking just like the man who did this to her. I was reminded of it every day I was in that home. As was she. "So, at eleven, I decided enough was enough. I left to find him." His voice lowered "I left to hunt him down and rip out his heart."

His tone hardened and held a distinct edge. It was remembered pain and harshness that sliced through every word he spoke. And each syllable cut me, leaving a permanent scar on my soul. He was a child, nothing more than a child looking to kill his sperm donor. I, unfortunately, knew that kind of hate. However, I never let it take me over like Cannon had. I was making excuses for him, possibly because on so many levels we were so much alike.

I wanted to say something, anything. But, nothing I could say would make him feel better or change how he felt. So I said nothing.

"Shortly after I left, she met and married Lachlan's father. I was in some ways happy for her. Now she had the power to live a normal life because I was gone."

"What about you? Where was your normal life?" I could hear the emotion in my voice and there was no way for me to disguise it.

His lips twitched slightly at the corners. It was a macabre smile that didn't reach his eyes. He stalked over and stood in front of me. I looked up and met his dark eyes.

"This story doesn't have a happy ending, Addison. I don't deserve one. So, get the thought of your happily ever after out of your head." His words were honest. That fact hurt me more than I was willing to admit.

"I traveled around Scotland, trying to find the man I called *father* for a few years. My mother had known his name, as he was employed by her father, and I knew I looked like him, so I searched for him. I found out when I was thirteen that he was in what is now Russia, but then it was called Muscovy. So, that's the direction I went." He sounded so normal speaking about himself as a child, traveling around the world to kill a man. Though if I could have found a way to kill my uncle for what he'd done to me, I would have.

"It didn't take me long to find him. Though when I did…" he paused, "…he wasn't what I expected."

"What do you mean?" I asked.

Cannon shifted and slowly, as though not to frighten me, sat down just to my left. I turned slightly to face him.

"He wasn't old and pathetic like I expected. He was young." His gaze was distant and his accent seemed to get thicker as he spoke.

"Young?" I asked, not really understanding what he was saying.

"He was the one who turned me. He was a vampire."

I think my eyes bulged out of my head and my jaw nestled firmly against the floor.

"When I found him, he was in some back alley, feeding. He killed the poor girl he was draining. I was frozen in shock. All I could do was blink at her pale form hanging limply in his arms, blood trickling down her body. His mouth firmly pressed against her throat. I was transfixed. I hated him. But, at that moment, I was conflicted."

"Conflicted?" I was the one who was transfixed, hell.

"I had heard horror stories about what he was all throughout my childhood. I think he was changed after he raped my mother, but the lore of my kind was a bedtime story meant to scare children into not walking the streets alone. I was torn. I wanted to kill him, but I knew I never could, not while he was so strong and I so young and weak."

"So what did you do?" I shifted on the bed to face him more fully. I was physically and metaphorically on the edge of my seat. I felt like a kid hearing a story for the first time. The only thing that could possibly make this story better would be popcorn with extra butter and a half melted Icee.

"I waited until he finished his meal. He dropped the girl on the ground and walked toward me." His tone was that of someone who was reliving a fond memory. Had I been him, I would have piddled in my pants. Hell, I wasn't far from it now.

"I had been looking for this man, hating him from afar my whole life. I had lost my fear of him long ago. He eyed me and brushed past me. I knew he had no idea who I was. I yelled after him that I wanted to be like him. He turned to me and told me to 'vernut'sya k materi sinitsy vashikh.'"

I looked up at him, not knowing what the hell he'd just said.

"He told me to go back to my mother's tit." He laughed so forcefully it sounded raw and without emotion. "I then informed him that I would kill him in his sleep and drink his blood as an afterthought."

I was shocked at how hard and emotionless his words were. I had no doubt that he had said them then much the same as he did to me right now. But, it gave me a glimpse into who he was then. He was a child ruined by everyone around him. A father who raped his mother and a mother who hated him for ruining her life. I didn't want to understand him. I didn't want to have this as common ground. But I did. I knew how it felt to be hated. Had it not been for Cannon finding me when he did — holy shit. Cannon had saved me. The revelation nearly knocked me over. I belatedly realized that he wasn't talking.

"Sorry," I muttered.

"I had clearly intrigued him. He told me to meet him there again the next night. I did. I watched him kill again. This went on for what seemed like years. He killed countless women and a few men. Sometimes he raped the women first, rather than feeding just to cause them pain. And I stood there and did nothing to help them." He spat the word *nothing* as though he couldn't stand it being in his mouth for one more second. It was the first negative tone I'd heard. Maybe he was redeemable.

"Their blood covers and stains my soul just as much, if not more, than his." His tone was so laced with hatred it was clear he thought he was just like his father.

"I began to learn what he liked. It became my job over the next few years to find him his feeders. So you see, Addison, I died long before I was turned. I've always been dead inside."

There was the difference between Cannon and Lachlan. Lachlan hated what he'd become. Cannon was born hating what and who he was, but he reveled in the creature he'd become. My heart hurt for the unloved boy he used to be. But, that would do me no good sitting next to the man he was forced to become.

"I got to know my father and he'd always been a monster. Every moment of his life. When he changed me, I was twenty-nine ... or eight. I don't recall the exact age. But when I woke from death, I didn't kill him like I thought I would. I wanted to use him. I wanted to learn everything I could. That's what I did until I heard Lachlan had come of age. That's when I told my father who I was. He just laughed at me, saying that he thought one of the hundred or so bastards would track him down. Then, he told me that he was proud of me because I had become just like him. That's when I snapped. I ripped his head off his shoulders slowly. I enjoyed every moment of it. I often think back to that kill and wish I could do it over and over again."

I reached up and ran a finger along his cheek. I had no idea why I did this. Maybe it was one broken soul knowing another. He snatched my hand away from his face and held it in a firm grip.

"I'm not human, Addison. I haven't been since I was a child. You can't fix what I am. But," he looked at my fingers protruding from his fist, "with you I feel."

I had no time to think or even respond to him before he placed my ring finger in his mouth. He sucked the tip lightly before he nicked it on his razor-sharp fang. Heat bloomed and spread throughout my whole body, just from that mere contact. Someone who sounded a lot like me groaned. It wasn't me though. I hoped anyway.

"Stand up," he snarled. Not in anger, but in hunger.

Slowly, I stood up, never taking my gaze from his. He too stood and walked behind me. I had to will myself not to turn to face him. He brushed the hair away from my neck, and I couldn't help but shake. I tried like hell to calm my body so it wouldn't respond to him. I was failing. He'd opened up to me. He had let me see his horrors. He kept reminding me he wasn't human, but he had never seemed more human than when he was telling me his story.

"Are you cold?" I could hear from his words he knew I wasn't.

"No." My tone was husky. As in, I thought for a moment I had turned into Stevie Nicks.

He placed a hand low on my belly and pressed himself against me. I could feel his rigid erection against my lower back. With the other hand, he tilted my head to the side.

His lips brushed my sensitive skin, setting it on fire. I didn't want to want this. I didn't need this, so I shouldn't want it.

All thoughts of needing and wanting were chased away by the searing pain of his bite. The pain died and quickly turned to immeasurable pleasure.

His hand that rested low on my abdomen pulled up the hem of the shirt and dipped lower. My breathing became ragged. I could stop this. I had the ability. His finger brushed my sex and any more thought of stopping this took a swan dive out the window. His masterful fingers parted my folds as he got his first feel of me.

He groaned against my skin at the first contact of my wet flesh. His finger circled my clit, but never touched it. I couldn't even arch to him. He drew from my neck, sending yet more heat to course through me and settled in a wet rush at my core.

"Can-" I didn't get the chance to finish my protest or encouragement before he sank his finger fully inside of me. His thumb found my swollen little clit and he began his slow seduction. I could feel myself being hurtled to my climax. There was no fighting this.

He withdrew his fangs just long enough to say one word: "Come." He buried another finger inside of me at the same time as his fangs penetrated me again. It was as though I needed that word or permission. I flew apart. My body shook and I could feel my sex clenching, trying to draw him deeper inside of me. My vision actually blurred, and I might have blacked out for a moment. His thumb never slowed its assault on my throbbing clit. I tried to push him away, as it was becoming too much for me to take.

"Please," I whispered. Oh sweet release, but I had

no idea if I wanted him to do more or to stop.

He pulled away from both my neck and my sex, turning me in his arms. His eyes were black as coal and a drop of my blood dripped down his full lip. He raised his finger to catch the stray droplet. His digit still glistened with my wetness. He sucked it in his mouth. After what seemed like twenty minutes, he smiled and grabbed my chin between his finger and thumb.

"Next time, you're mine, Addison. And you know it."

I did know it. And I had no idea how I felt about it. Still, that sorted, insane part of me wondered? No, hoped, he would try now.

He walked over to the door and glanced at me over his shoulder.

"Go home and pack. We leave for Chicago tomorrow." He opened the door, with no further explanation.

Oh hell. This was either going to be very good or very bad. And I had no idea which I was hoping for.

Chapter Twelve

Before leaving Cannon's, I went to see Theo again. I couldn't apologize enough. He seemed to be doing better though. It seemed like he was healing pretty quickly. I wondered if it had been Cannon's blood, but didn't really have time to think too long. I had a short amount of time to get all of my shit together.

My run home had been, well, thoughtful. I could not get Cannon out of my head. Everything he'd been through. How he became what he was. Shit, it was a wonder that he could come out on the other side at all. He was a child who was forced to do things I couldn't even fathom. Yet, he'd told me that I made him feel. Feel what? What the hell did that mean?

As I approached my apartment, I sighed. There, sitting by the door was a large flower box. I thought about just trashing it, but there was a note attached to it. I slid the piece of paper out and opened it.

Addison,

You looked so beautiful the other night. So wet. You got me so hard.

What. The. Actual. Fuck? I don't think an army or even rabid bears could have stopped me from getting the hell in my apartment. My heart was beating like a wild thing and my skin was covered with sweat. I slammed the door behind me and tried to will my heart to slow down. I dropped the note on the floor as though it were covered with a hundred tiny spiders. I did not have time for this bull crap. I took in several large gulps of air. After a few moments my heart rate slowed and I was able to think a little bit more rationally.

I had to call Darryl and let him know I was likely going to be gone for a few days. I needed to pack. *Wait, how long will we be gone?* I needed to call Cannon and ask. I needed to not think about the box I left sitting outside my door or the note that would surely turn into a velociraptor and destroy my couch. There was a whole lot of shit I needed to do. None of it I wanted to do.

I held my phone in my hand, since the damn shirt I was wearing didn't have any pockets. I side-stepped the note laying harmlessly on the floor, giving it a wide birth.

I dialed Cannon.

"Couldn't stay away too long, huh, pusher?" His smooth low voice licked along my nerves.

"Cannon, how long do I need to pack for?" I asked, clearly dodging his line of questioning.

"Two or three days at most."

"Okay. thanks. I-" I was cut off by the line going dead. I pulled the phone from my ear and looked at the blank screen staring back at me.

"Ass bucket," I scolded the phone.

I dialed Darryl. There was no answer so I left a message. I glanced at the clock on the microwave. He would be in the middle of a class, so he would get it later.

I grabbed a bag and tossed my clothes and other essentials in. I walked into the bathroom to change and caught my refection in the mirror.

Staring back at me was someone I hardly recognized. I looked tired. I needed a shower and had dark purple circles running just under my eyes that fanned out into a deep red. My skin was covered in bruises. But, that wasn't what caught me off-guard.

I felt guilty. I had this clenching in the pit of my stomach that threatened to double me over. I would say I had no idea why I had this feeling when I saw myself, but I knew perfectly well. It was everything I had done with Cannon. It was everything I had allowed to happen all while Lachlan was somewhere in some fucked-up mess. All the while, I was creating a shitstorm of my own.

I tried hard as hell to not hate myself, but I had a feeling that if I gave in with Cannon, I very well might.

I turned my back on my reflection and walked to the shower. I needed to get clean and sleep. I needed to brace myself for this trip. I needed to brace myself for Cannon. Most of all, I needed to get ready to fight everything my body seemed to want. Talk about a fight. Hell, it would be a full-on, knock-down, kicking, screaming, hair-pulling brawl.

Sleep was elusive. I tossed and turned, failing to find sleep, finally rolling over and slipping my hands under my pillow. My fingertips grazed something hard. What the ... Oh. I remembered the little red journal. Sitting up, I pulled it out. My room was dark and I was warm, sleep should have come easily. But the compulsion to read this particular book was pretty overwhelming. Focusing on the light switch, I pulsed my power. Nothing happened. After four more tries, I gave up and walked my happy ass out of bed. Okay, I more or less stumbled, as I left my shoes and clothes on the floor.

I walked back to my warm bed and picked up the small leather booklet. The first entry was dated just two weeks before Lachlan and I met. The first thing I noticed was that for someone who grew up in the time of calligraphy and fancy writing, his penmanship was shit. I was, however, grateful that it was in English.

Today has been like most of the others since coming to Atlanta, filled with the bullshit of my brother. Not that life was any better in Chicago. Life has become dull and draws on and on. I feed to stay alive but I, honestly, have gotten no joy from it in some time. Maybe this means I'm set to have the fate of other old vampires. I can only hope.

That's where the first entry ended. What the hell did that mean? Well, I mean I get the whole "woe is me, I wish the grass were so emo it would cut itself" kind of vibe, but that last part, about the old vampires. What the hell did that even mean? I skipped the next few entries and went to the day he and I met. I know, I know, I shouldn't, but it was like the button they tell you not to press. I couldn't help it!

Addison Fitzpatrick. She was five foot nothing and has an attitude in spades. There is no way I will be able to work with her. Seeing Cannon on her like that tonight though, I wanted to rip his throat out. Not that I didn't always want to, but seeing him on HER brought out the monster in me. Now, I'm forced to work with her. I will have to fight to keep my fangs and my cock to myself. But, damn the girl made me feel. I haven't felt anything in so long. I just want to hold on to that. I'm so fucked.

I felt like a voyeur. I closed the book and tossed it across the room. I just couldn't read about Lachlan while having increased feelings for Cannon. God, I didn't know what I was expecting. Maybe to not be so damn conflicted. I flopped back in the bed. My head was swimming with thoughts of Lachlan and images of Cannon.

This is going to be a long night. I hoped that the flight tomorrow went off without a hitch because I really just wanted something to be easy and smooth.

"Wait. What do you mean we're driving? That's like ten fucking hours!"

This had been my question I'd asked some nine hours ago. Cannon had given me some incredulous answer about the sun and a plane not being safe. In the end, while the sun was a concern, I knew it had to do with control. And because Cannon was a controlling, self-righteous bastard, I was forced to sit in a stuffy car with him for ten freaking hours. This was listed just under water-boarding in the "how to torture" handbook. Thank God I could sleep just about anywhere, because I spent the better part of the trip unconscious.

Cannon, as far as I could tell, never slept. All he did was brood. I had no idea just what we were walking into in Chicago, but it clearly had him in a mood.

"Cannon?"

"What?" he snapped.

"What the hell is wrong with you?" I couldn't help the fire in my tone.

"Look, I haven't seen Merriam in a number of years. The last time I did, we didn't really end on good terms. She's more powerful than I am and this could all end poorly. I have a lot more to think about right now than your silly infatuation with my brother."

"Whoa there, killer. A simple 'I'm having that male vampire time of the month' would have sufficed. Quick, someone find him some chocolate-laced blood!" Had I just said that, out loud? *Oh shit.*

"Addison, let me break this down for you." His fists clenched and unclenched. Clearly, he was trying to reign in his temper. His mouth was set in a hard line and his eyes were deepening to black. "I have to see a more powerful vampire than myself. The only reason

I retain power is because she allows it. And I'm forced to bring you along, not because I want to, but because knowing you, you would just find a way to be there, in turn killing yourself."

There was something frantic in his tone. Was he afraid?

Wait. I was not that big of a fuck-up, was I? I thought back and cringed. I may have a slight impulse-control problem.

"It also doesn't help the situation that Merriam wants to see you." He added this last statement as though it was an afterthought. My eyes flew open in disbelief.

"I'm sorry, what?" I scoffed, nearly choking on the words as they flew out of my mouth.

Cannon didn't have time to respond, because the car stopped outside of a large hotel. The driver exited and opened Cannon's door. The windows were tinted, so I couldn't really get a good look at the building, but it was incredibly bright. Cannon got out and offered me a hand. Night had completely taken over the sky, but the hotel was so brightly lit that you couldn't really tell what time of day it was. All I could do was blink and let what I was seeing sink in.

The hotel was white with a number of large

windows. It wasn't the largest building, by far, but it screamed money. There were two enormous statues of lions situated on either side of the large entrance. The light from the lobby spilled out from the doors and windows, casting a bright white, nearing blue tone to everything. There was a bite in the air that made me glad I thought to bring a jacket. Though I still felt underdressed.

Cannon had his standard suit that cost more than I made in a year. Everyone we passed, from the bellhops to the guests, looked to be made of money. And then there was me. I had on jeans and a white, long-sleeved T-shirt. I felt like the Wal-Mart special. It didn't help that I felt like I was being stared at, and not in a good way.

Cannon made his way up to the front desk and didn't say a damn word. The sharply dressed woman blushed and typed in a few things in her computer. After handing him an envelope she scurried away, giggling. *What the hell?* She slid her eyes to me and gave me a onceover. Her lip curled upward in disgust. Just as I was about to go all Speedy Gonzales on her ass, Cannon turned around, shaking his head, and ushered me to the elevator. Every single employee that we passed seemed to glance up at him, then turn around and run or scuttle away. They were acting like he was some kind of god, well, that or a devil. I was betting the latter.

We stepped into the elevator and dear sweet mother of ravioli, the damn thing was opulent. I mean the whole place was, but it only hit me just how pricey this place must be when we stepped in. I bet rent in that damn elevator would be what I paid in a year at my apartment.

If I thought the elevator and lobby were stunning, they didn't hold a candle to the room itself. Once Cannon opened the door, all I could do was look from one crazy-ass expensive thing to the next. I felt the need to keep my hands in my pockets for fear of touching something and accidentally breaking it. One freaking chip would be like, poof, there goes a year's rent.

Wandering into the bedroom, I found myself not really understanding what exactly I was looking at.

"Cannon!" I called. I felt him pressed against my back, his cool skin penetrating the thin cotton of my shirt. Swallowing I croaked, "There's only one bed in here."

"What's your point?" His voice was so low I felt more than heard his words bounce off my skin.

"Uh ... um ... I mean, Cannon." I hated having him

near me. Okay, not hated, but hated how my body wanted him so damn badly.

Turning me to face him, he whispered, "Addison. I would never do something you didn't want."

"Well, my body may want you, but it doesn't need you." The words may have been forced, but they were true. At least that's what I wanted to believe. My heart was racing.

"Addison." He had a way of saying my name that made it sound naughty and forbidden.

I raised my eyebrows in response. I really didn't trust my voice at that point.

"In life, we have things we need. But then there are the things, Addison…" He brushed his lips against my neck. His hands slipped around my waist, cutting off any way of escape. Though I wasn't sure I would run if given the chance.

His mouth moved to my ear and I could feel his cool breath as he spoke, "There are things you want. You have to be big enough to admit what it is that you want."

He pulled away, meeting my eyes. His gaze was nearly completely black and I could see the white tips of his fangs. I tried to ignore the ache that was building low in my belly.

"Now the question is, Addison, what do you want?"

He didn't give me time to think or respond. He simply left me there panting in his wake. *Why does he do crap like that? Fuck this.*

"Cannon!" I yelled after him.

Sauntering back into the room, he replied, "Yes?"

"Why do you do that?" I was irritated. No, I was pissed. He was the most hot-and-cold person I'd ever met.

"Because you're not ready to admit you want me." His lips curved up into a smug-ass smile. What pissed me off more was that I knew with every part of me that he was right.

I narrowed my eyes at him, but just as I was about to have the wittiest of all comebacks, he held up a hand as if to tell me to shut up. Did he think he was speaking with a child? Or some weak-minded female? Clearly he'd lost his damn mind.

"Go to hell, Cannon," I growled. I had no damn idea why I continued to provoke a being that would rend me in two with a snap of his fingers. Maybe because it chafed me to think people thought I was weak or insubstantial. *I am a force.*

Walking toward me, he snarled, "Have you ever thought it might be a good idea for you to be afraid of me?" He came within an inch of me. I could feel his anger pouring off him in waves. He didn't give me time to answer before starting again.

"Merriam is stronger than me. If she decides to kill you, I could do nothing to stop her." I couldn't meet his eyes. He grabbed my chin and pulled my face up to his.

"Are you hearing me? Because you take pleasure in infuriating me. While I tolerate it, she won't. Damn it, Addison, you need to listen to me and take everything I'm about to say to heart. Otherwise, I can't save you from her." His words were hurried and his eyes searched mine. It seemed as though my next words mattered to him, a lot.

"Okay." I swallowed what I really wanted to say. This wasn't the time to puff out my chest and explain how strong I was. He clearly was looking to keep my mouth from saying something that would get me killed.

Releasing his grip on my chin, he took a step back and eyed me from head to toe. I then looked at myself and glanced back to him. He was frowning. All I could do was shrug. I didn't see what the issue was.

"We need to get you ready. You … don't look your best."

"Wait. What? Ready for what? It's nearly 10 p.m.

And I look fine for someone who just spent forty hours in a car." Okay it was like ten, but it felt like forty.

"We meet her tonight. In two hours to be exact. You have about an hour to get ready and learn how to keep your mouth shut." He raised his eyebrows at me, then continued, "Think you can handle that?"

"Uh … Yup!" I said in a bright tone. I also added a thumbs up for extra reassurance. I was actually able to say that without laughing, choking on the words, or getting struck by lightning.

"We have a lot of work ahead of us," he commented as he dialed a number on the hotel phone.

We were just meeting a vampire who would kill the shit out of me. How much work could that be? It's not like I slept with her consort or anything … Oh wait.

Chapter Thirteen

annon, is this really necessary?" I called over my shoulder. I stood in front of a large mirror, and staring back at me was someone I didn't know. Okay, when Gen had dolled me all up I looked, well, provocative. Not that there's anything wrong with that; it's just not me. Still, I at least looked my age. This though … I turned, keeping my eyes glued to the strange person … was insane.

I wore a dress the same deep blue as the outer ring of my eyes. It was long-sleeved and pooled around my feet. The material felt like a second skin hugging every inch of my body, including my throat. There was a deep V on the back of the dress that dipped so near my rump I was afraid to bend over for fear of a wardrobe malfunction. The damn dress looked like it was painted on. It was sexy without showing hardly any skin, well aside from my back. My hair was piled atop my head in a crazy explosion of blonde curls. Had I done it, it would have looked like I'd just been caught in a category five hurricane, but the hairstylist made it look elegant.

I was twenty-five, though I always looked about eighteen. That moment, in that dress, I looked like a grown-ass woman. As amazing as I knew I looked, I felt like a fish out of water. Hell, I was even making that mouth open, gasping-for-air look.

"Addison, you look beautiful. Is what necessary?" he crooned as I felt him run a cold finger down my spine. I had to stifle a shiver.

"All of this? I feel like we're going to the opera." I gestured to my reflection.

"Yes, it is. Now, do you remember the rules of the night?" he questioned for the hundredth time.

I let out an exasperated sigh and rolled my eyes as I replied, "Yes, Cannon. You've only made me say them fifty times."

He raised his brows expectantly.

Groaning, I uttered the rules, "I will only speak when spoken to." Okay, I would give it the old college try. Really, I would. "I cannot look at Merriam for longer than five seconds. Because she might entrance me and then tell me to go jump off a cliff, then I would have to." Okay, that last one, I would not have an issue with. "I should not show my throat to anyone under any circumstances."

"And…" He knew I had full knowledge of what his last rule was. He continued to run his damn finger slowly up and down my back. I was having a hard time thinking.

"And … I will not talk back to, question, or undermine anyone, especially you or Merriam." I took a step forward and then ducked past Cannon.

"You're not going to have a problem doing that last one, will you?" he asked, eyeing me.

"Who me? Never." My tone being very clear that I just could not believe he would think otherwise. In the end I was totally lying and knew I would have every issue complying to my last Cannon-imposed rule. "I don't know Cannon; it almost seems like I would be doing you a favor by following these rules." I quipped while looking down at my nails.

"No, you'd be doing you a favor by not dying. That's the best I'm going to get, isn't it?" he asked, clearly knowing damn well what the answer would be.

"Pretty much."

He shook his head and headed toward the door.

"Cannon?" I asked.

Turning to face me, hand resting on the knob, he arched a brow at me.

"How will this help us find Lachlan?"

• 1 7 5 •

He flinched at the mention of his brother's name. It was nearly imperceptible, but for a being who was often motionless, it was a major tell. Though, I had no idea what it meant.

"She could possibly tell us just what we're up against and how to track it. But, you need to come to terms with the idea that he could be dead."

And, just like that, a lump formed in my throat and a vise tightened around my stomach. That was absolutely not something I could come to terms with. I had no idea how I felt about Lachlan or Cannon, but I knew I would be devastated if either of them were dead. I shook my head to try to rid the swirling thoughts. I needed to figure everything out. But now wasn't the time.

"You ready?" he asked, turning his back to me. All I could do was nod, even though he couldn't see me. I wasn't ready. Not even a little bit. Fake it until you make it, right?

After I got involved with Cannon, I watched just about every vampire movie there was. I know, I know, a reliable source of information, right? Yeah, I think I did myself a disservice. I've never actually seen one wear the ruffle shirts or have long black claws. Still, I couldn't help pull up the old movies as we approached Merriam's home. Wait ... lair? Fortress of solitude? Crypt?

Anyway, I guess I was expecting see a castle like in *Nasferatu* or an antebellum mansion like in *Interview with the Vampire*. Cannon told me it would be a large house, so I guess my imagination ran a little wild. But no imagining or thinking could have really prepared me for what I saw.

When we pulled up, there was a tall iron gate. There was no intercom, but there had to have been cameras or something I couldn't see, because the gate doors swung open allowing us entrance.

"Addison." Cannon's voice broke whatever spell the ornate gate held over me. I flicked my eyes to his. "One more thing." He paused for what I could only assume was dramatic effect.

"Okay?" I hedged.

"Don't eat anything." My eyebrows raised at his words. What was this, the fairy kingdom? Would I turn into a rat?

"Okay, I'll bite. Why?" And no, the punnyness of my words wasn't lost on me.

"I'm not dumb enough to think that in the time Merriam has been awake, she hasn't heard of you and

Lachlan. That being said, if she could take you out by a simple poison, well, I wouldn't put it past her."

For fuck's sake, did everyone know and care about who was in, or had been in, my bed?

"Great, even people who haven't met me hate me. Sounds about right," I quipped. I was trying to make light of the situation, but Cannon's features only hardened.

"Addison, please take this seriously. We are going into that house knowing that I may not be able to protect you." As he spoke, his words got harsher. *Damn him.* All of this time spent with him was softening me toward him and everything inside of me was pushing to rebel. Everything except my libido, that slut had other plans.

"Addison!" Cannon snapped.

I looked up at him.

"Sorry, I know, Cannon. I'll do my best not to be…" I trailed off as the "house," as Cannon put it, came into view. *Okay there is not one dictionary on the planet that would classify this as a house.* Compound? Possibly. Versailles? Would be a whole lot closer.

The house was in the shape of a U. In the middle there was a large fountain. As much as the massive size may have shocked me, just how rundown and forgotten the place was shocked me even more. I mean, I'm sure she could afford a groundskeeper. The real question was, why had it been so neglected?

The car jolted slightly as it was put into park. My mouth went instantly dry. I wasn't scared. *Clearly I love lying to myself.*

Getting out of the car, the strong scent of rotting things assailed my nose, causing my eyes to water. *What the hell is that smell?* I was afraid to speak. I feared that if I opened my mouth, I would taste the rancid scent. I really didn't want to chance that.

Walking toward us was a tall African-American man with dreadlocks that hung down to the middle of his back. As he closed the distance, I was able to take him in.

He was tall. Like Cannon tall. But, he was a hell of a lot broader. He looked to be a wall of a man, yet his facial features were delicate. His jaw was wide, but his cheeks were sharp and high. His nose fit his delicate features to a T. His lips were so full, it made me wonder if he could speak around them. He was stunning, and pulling everything together were the impossibly dark pools he called eyes. They were almost entirely the color of obsidian and shined like black stars.

The man stopped a few feet from Cannon. A smirk spread across his dark features.

Bowing, the man intoned, "Welcome to the would-be king of our kind." He had an accent of some kind. I couldn't quite put my finger on it though. It sounded like a type of British, but not really.

Cannon's fists, which rested at his sides, clenched and unclenched. The man's eyes were trained on me. I had no fear like I thought I would though. I had to bite my tongue.

The man was wearing a white shirt and tan linen pants. The shirt lay open, exposing his chiseled chest. He had some kind of brand that had been burned into his flesh a long time ago. I couldn't help but stare at it, trying to make out its shape. All I was able to do was make out scales. My eyes flicked to his. His own were pinched in amusement. I tried not to flush, failing miserably.

"Polo, where is your mistress? I thought she had a tight leash on you."

Polo's eyes brightened in a spark of anger before they narrowed on Cannon.

"Oh, but Cannon. She said I was to attend to your pet." His pink tongue licked his full bottom lip and I had to stifle a shudder. "And, while I wasn't at all happy, now having seen her I think I have all kinds of things we could do…" His words fell silent as he looked me over from head to toe.

His eyes bore a hole into me wherever they landed. I swallowed hard. I knew I couldn't be left alone with this vampire. I would be forced to kill him and I didn't think that would be very good for public relations.

"Oh, South Africa!" I blurted without thinking. *Shit!* My hands flew to my mouth but not before I saw the smirk that seemed to be permanently plastered over Polo's face widen into a bright smile. Cannon, however, wasn't amused at all. His hand flew out and grabbed my upper arm. He gave it a quick squeeze to indicate his extreme disapproval. Had his eyes been lasers, I'd be so dead. All I could do was shrug. But hey, at least I placed his accent.

Polo burst out in loud guffaws of laughter.

"Oh, Cannon, this is going to be," he paused and ran his tongue along one of his gleaming white fangs, "fun." The way he said the word made a shiver run up my spine.

"Polo, I think I hear your master calling you. How about you be a good lap dog and heel."

Polo's lips peeled away from his teeth in a snarl. He turned, without a word, and stalked away. Clearly, there was a history with these two. I opened my mouth to ask about it, but Cannon gave me a pointed look. I shut my mouth with an audible clack. Maybe speaking wasn't wise. I really did not want to push my luck.

Polo reached the ornately carved doors and turned to face us.

"Please, won't you come in?" he asked between gritted teeth.

Cannon's hand moved from my arm to my lower back. He applied light pressure as we both walked forward. I had a distinct feeling that we were walking into the lion's den, dressed in nothing but steak. And that was a look only Lady Gaga could pull off. At least I was good at one thing.

Running.

Chapter Fourteen

The inside of the house was something straight out of a foreclosure's worst nightmare. The outside was beautiful and looked as though when it was built someone took great care of how the structure would age. But the inside resembled the state of the yard. Overgrown and unkempt. There was a thick layer of dust and dirt covering nearly everything. There were sheets draped over every piece of furniture. The sconces that were placed on the walls worked, but they seemed to be on their last legs. The low glow of amber light flickered and really didn't illuminate much beyond the layers of grime.

"Waiting on the maid?" *Oh. Holy. Shit. I did not say that out loud.* I felt Cannon's fingers stiffen on my back.

Polo's low laughter filled the empty expanse of space to the brim. *Yeah, I said it.* Damnit, what was wrong with my brain-to-mouth filter?

"Addison, I know you enjoy infuriating me. But, could

you for once keep your mouth shut?" Cannon scolded me in my mind.

"Sorry, it just came out!"

I think I felt him roll his eyes.

Polo wove us through a maze of marble and mahogany-carved columns. Had the place been cleaned and restored a bit, it would have been jaw-dropping, but, as it stood, it was kind of lackluster.

We walked up on a large entryway that was sealed off by two large double doors.

All thought and observation was interrupted by a high-pitched shriek. The cry was laced with so much pain that I lunged forward on instinct. I couldn't go far, as Cannon's arm whipped out and he caught me around the waist.

"Calm the hell down. Remember, she wants to get a reaction from you." His statement bounced off the sides of my skull, creating a cacophony of words.

I was shaking, not for fear of myself, but for the person that scream came from. The cries of sheer pain and fear died down until I could only hear dull whimpers.

"Remember, she's not like Lachlan. Or even myself. She'll kill and not think twice about doing so. Even if it's for your benefit."

I didn't trust myself to put together a coherent

thought, so I just nodded. I glanced to Polo, who had a smug, knowing smile that caused the corners of his dark lips to raise slightly. I wanted to knock his perfect head right off his perfect shoulders.

Cannon was right. I had to control myself. This was all to get me to make a mistake, to give her a reason to kill me, or worse. I swallowed and injected every bit of iron I had into my spine. I could do this. I just had to try harder. *We have to find Lachlan,* I kept chanting in my mind and for once I didn't care if Cannon heard it or not.

Just as Cannon's arm relaxed, Polo slid open one of the massive doors.

The room was a stark contrast to the rest of the house. It looked to be clean and breathtakingly stunning. But, that wasn't what drew my attention — it was the twenty or so vampires, or what I assumed to be vampires, lining the walls. In the middle of the room, surrounded by those vampires, sat a woman cradling a limp form.

The woman looked up and met my eyes. I froze. There wasn't so much a force keeping me from moving, but the look that radiated from her gaze shocked the hell out of me. Her eyes looked completely dead. Even the smile that slowly appeared on her face brought no life to the dull, soft blue orbs. Her skin was the color of melted caramel, which should have made the corn-flower color of her eyes pop, but there was literally no life sparking behind them. It was eerie to see such a beautiful woman with no love of life backing her.

Is this what would happen to Cannon? Or Lachlan? Will they become so detached from being human that they lose all ability to live? Is this what Lachlan spoke of in his journal?

I glanced around to the vampires who lined the room. Their gazes were focused on the scene playing out on the floor. They didn't all look as dead as the woman on the floor, but they didn't have that spark I would associate with humanity.

My eyes returned to the woman on the floor. Her smile widened. There was a thick line of blood trick-ling from the corner of her mouth down her neck and fanning across her beautiful white dress. I didn't need to look at the form she cradled so delicately in her lap. I knew whoever it had been was now dead. Cannon was right. This was all a show for me. And because of that, whoever that had been was no more. Again, be-cause of me. I gritted my teeth to avoid saying or doing something stupid.

It didn't take me long to hate this woman. I refused

to name her, even though I knew perfectly well who she was. She couldn't have been more than twenty-two or three when she was turned. She had delicate features. A pinpoint nose, thin pink lips, and her hair was nearing a tight curling mass of black and amber strands. Between her features and her café ole skin, she should have been striking, but the eyes killed it. At least for me.

"Cannon. Look. You brought me a pet." She never took her eyes off of me. The light French accent found its way to coil around my throat. I inhaled a deep breath.

"Merriam. You're looking …" He paused, picking his words carefully. He finally settled on, " …well.". Knowing Cannon, I knew his words were a lie. An expression flashed across Merriam's face, but it was so fast I didn't have time to discern what it was.

She stood up, half giggling. The form I now identified as a young woman toppled to the floor with a dull thud. I flinched. I knew it would be shown as weakness, but I couldn't help it. I hoped the others didn't notice; it was a fleeting hope, as Merriam's gaze was trained on me, as though she were a hawk and I her prey.

I did my best not to look into her dead eyes, but it was hard. Harder than I thought it would be. I had to bite back a snippy comment just about every time I looked at the vampire.

She was slightly taller than me when she stood at her full height, though not by much. Short stature or not, she had a presence that commanded the whole room. Though I could see the others in the space, I bet I could hear a pin drop.

I felt myself staring into her eyes. I could feel her trying to do something, but other than a slight pressure in my mind, nothing happened. In that moment her amused features turned dark.

"She can't be entranced. How…" she trailed off, letting her eyes travel the length of me, "…unfortunate." Her tone was so dismissive that my eyes flew wide in incredulity.

"What's unfortunate is the state of this house. Haven't you heard of a Swiffer duster before?" *Oh fuck me.* I couldn't stop the words from coming out of my mouth. But, damnit, I had a hard time seeing this woman as a threat. I mean, I knew logically she could kill me without batting an eye, but really I could only see her as a catty female. Crazy, oh hell yes, but more catty.

I didn't dare look at Cannon. I knew he would be furious. Merriam, however, just smiled. Not a sweet smile, but a slight quark of her lips and a brief peek of her fangs. It was predatory. I did not fail to notice that her pointed little teeth were yet to retract.

She stalked closer to me, pacing a tight circle around Cannon and me. Though I knew it was really me she was evaluating.

"So, this is the creature MY Lachlan has been," she cocked her head as if in thought, "… infatuated with." She spat the words as though they were distasteful on her tongue. Wait, if she'd been in some kind of trance and not been in communication with Lachlan, how the hell would she know that?

Apparently, my confusion was clear. Because she scoffed, "His thoughts are muddled with thoughts of you. Such human thoughts."

Human thoughts? My heart began to pound.

"And being human. That's bad?" I couldn't help but ask.

"Having human emotions as a vampire is weak. And, yes. Humanity by definition is weakness."

"We aren't all weak." I knew when I said it how fragile the argument was, but I did not want this woman for whatever reason to see me as anything other than a forced to be reckoned with.

She laughed. "Oh? No? But, you aren't entirely human are you? Pusher."

Between gritted teeth I said, "More human than you'll ever be."

"Addison!" Cannon roared in indignation. He took a step closer to me. I knew that I had broken the rules but damnit, I was trying. Okay maybe I wasn't trying, maybe I was letting my impulses take over. I knew I was being dumb, but I couldn't seem to stop myself. Merriam held up a hand to stop him. That fucking vampire didn't move an inch.

"Everyone, leave. Except you." She pointed to me. I could barely make out the words, they were so low.

As if in one motion, the vampires lining the walls filed out. My gaze flicked to Cannon, who didn't so much as twitch in the direction of the exit.

Merriam's eyes turned red. Her lips curled back from her teeth and she hissed, "Cannon, that in no way excludes you!"

"I will not leave Addison." His tone was firm and even. If I was being honest, I really didn't want him to leave.

She slowly walked over to Cannon and reached up, wrapping her delicate fingers around his throat.

Cannon, much to my surprise, didn't do a thing.

With speed I'd never seen in someone other than myself, she jumped up on Cannon and sank her fangs in his throat. I took a step toward him.

"Stop," he called in my mind.

She nearly threw herself away from him just as fast. He toppled back a few steps before he was able to stop his momentum.

She had her head turned away from me. All I could hear was her cackling.

Between whoops of laughter she said, "Oh, Cannon. You're in deep with this one. You want what your brother has already had. You feel for her." She whirled to face us.

Her eyes were completely red and she could never be mistaken for anything other than a monster.

Her laugh stopped and she snarled, "And feeling makes you weak. I think, maybe I should take my place as master. What do you think?" This was the woman under the mask. This was the monster that lay beneath the facade of paint and frilly dresses. She was decayed to her very core.

"That's not why we are here," Cannon growled back.

And like a light switch, her eyes brightened.

"Oh, yes. But, I want to hear from her what she wants."

God isn't that the million-dollar question.

"I want to find Lachlan. I want to save him."

She shook her head.

"No, what do you want?" I had no idea what she wanted me to say.

"I-I don't know…" That really was the truth. I simply had no idea what it was I wanted.

"Now that you're being honest. Let's talk." She turned and walked to a door just to the left of the large room. Cannon followed her. In turn, I did the same thing.

"Cannon, what did she mean by-"

"Not now, Addison," he snapped.

This whole meeting hadn't really been what I expected, though I'm not sure what I'd thought was going to happen.

The door led to a small, nearly hidden room with three chairs and a small wooden table in the center. The room was draped in rich, red fabric that seemed to drip from the ceiling to the floor, making it look less like fabric and more like wax.

Atop the small table was a plate piled about three rows high with beautifully glazed donuts. My mouth watered, but I resisted. *How the flying hell did she know I love them?*

"Shall we negotiate?" She eyed me, but I knew the question was for Cannon.

"Yes. You know the information I want."

"Yes, yes." She waved at him, dismissing the statement. "Where is MY consort? And just what is it that has him?" She made sure she said the word *MY* in such a way that I knew she meant it.

He wasn't yours while his mouth was on my-

"Yes, Merriam. And what is it you want in return?" Cannon asked, cutting my thoughts off completely. His hands gripped the arms of the chair he was sitting in. If he clutched them any tighter, they would explode in a cloud of splinters.

"I thought he was YOUR consort? Wouldn't you want to help us find him?"

Her face turned cold at my words.

"Listen close, deary," she hissed her words. "I give nothing for free. As much as I would miss that beautiful body of his, it can be replaced."

I gritted my teeth and had to bite my tongue because the only words I knew I would say would come from jealousy.

"What do you want for the information?" Cannon asked, attempting to get her attention back on him.

"Two things. I want her," she nodded to me, "to never contact Lachlan again."

Well fuck that.

"And?" I blinked at Cannon in astonishment. Like fucking hell I would do that.

"I want a taste of her." My eyes nearly popped out of my head. *I'm sorry, say what now?*

"Both of those are up to her. I cannot answer."

Both of them peered at me, waiting for me to say something. *Hell, I have no idea what I will say.*

"If he contacts me, I won't stop it. As far as me contacting him…" I didn't want to agree to this. I didn't know how I even could. Everything around me seemed to be chipping away at my already damaged heart; soon there would be nothing left, just a sliver of what used to beat within me.

"I agree." There it went. That little part dying. I pushed back all the pain those two words brought. Nothing mattered, only saving Lachlan. "I'll let you have one sip from my wrist. After you tell us everything."

Her lips twitched and her eyes flicked from the natural dead blue to the vibrant red.

"It's done," was all she said. I felt like there was weight with her words. Weight I wasn't sure I understood. Not yet, anyway.

Chapter Fifteen

Would you like something to eat?"

I narrowed my eyes at her. *For the love of all that is holy I am going to strangle her.* We'd been here for about an hour and all we had managed was having to decipher her fucking riddles. Now we sat here waiting on Polo to return with her diary. According to Merriam, she conveniently couldn't remember this epic fight we spoke of.

"No thanks, I'm good." It was hard to keep the annoyance out of my voice. Damn her, my eyes slid to the sugary confections. I didn't want to say no, but Cannon had warned me.

Prior to getting clean, I'd developed an obsession with the yeasty goodness that was donuts, but as my sponsor informed me, it's common among opiate addicts to crave sweets. I shook my head to focus on the situation at hand.

She shrugged, but, seeming to have an idea, her face lit up and a smile caused her lips to twitch upward.

"Cannon, would you like to eat?"

I glanced to him. His eyes flickered dark for a moment before returning. He was hungry. He refused to feed before we left the hotel, saying he didn't want me any weaker than I was.

"No, I-"

"I insist. You look parched. I'm sure I have a human you could-"

"No," he cut her off firmly. This had been the first time I'd heard Cannon be firm and resolute with her.

She narrowed her eyes. "Cannon, you know how I love to watch you feed. Please indulge me."

He looked at me fully. I could feel his hunger pressing against skin. I swallowed. I was not at all comfortable with this.

"I'm sure our little Addison would oblige," she added as though she forgot to ask for special sauce on her hamburger.

Looking at her cold, glowing red eyes, I replied, "If I do this, you get no taste of my blood." I was not about to be fed on by two vampires.

Her jaw clenched causing her features to harden. Her lips parted and I could see her small white fangs. "Deal."

"Addison, you don't have to do this." His voice even mentally was rough.

"Cannon, I just want this to be over. And if this means she won't get a taste of my blood then so be it."

Cannon's eyes flooded with black. He wanted this so badly I'm sure he could taste it. I couldn't say the same. I wondered why she wanted this. Looking at Cannon, I tried to decipher if he knew, but the only thing I saw reflected back at me was his hunger.

"Come," he rasped.

I got up and walked over to him slowly.

"How do you want me?" I said this mentally for a number of reasons.

"Straddle me. She won't let me take your arm. She gets off on this."

Yet so did he. And, if I were being honest …Well, fuck honesty.

I hiked up my long dress and sat astride him. His hands slid to my ass and he pulled me closer to him. I could feel his firm erection press against my belly. I swallowed, hard.

Once he had me in the position he wanted, he moved his hand to the cloth high on my neck. His eyes never left mine. They were pulling me in, trapping me in place. I hated how he could pin me in place with just a look.

"Cannon. Please don't make this-" I tried to plead

with him not to make this sexual. Not here. Not now. My words were cut off by the cool brush of his lips against my throat. The feel of his tongue against my skin lit my skin on fire. This was the last place I wanted to do this. This was the last thing-

I felt his fangs slice into my neck. I had to bite down on my tongue to keep from moaning. My hands slipped to the back of his head and I instinctively pulled him closer. One of his hands slipped to the back of my neck and the other still rested firmly on my ass.

With every draw of his mouth and lap of his tongue I found it increasingly difficult to hold back my moans. I had to force myself not to rock against him.

He dug his hand into my ass at the same moment he bit deeper and that was nearly my undoing. I couldn't stifle the moan. I could barely contain my composure.

"Cannon. Please. Not here." My voice sounded weak even to me.

I felt him inhale. Something I knew he really didn't need to do. I didn't need to ask or wonder why he did it. I knew. He was trying to take in the scent of my arousal. And, despite myself, I was painfully turned on.

"Cannon." It came out a moan but I meant it to be pleading. I began rocking against his hardness. I tried

like hell to stop, but couldn't seem to remember why I needed to.

Without warning, his hands slipped to my upper arms and he withdrew his fangs with a snarl. My vision was still hazy and I couldn't really understand why he'd stopped.

I lowered my lips to his. I had no idea why I felt the need to kiss him, but I didn't think I could have stopped myself even if I'd wanted to. His lips were firm at first. Surprised, maybe? Then they softened and opened slightly. I could taste the metallic tang of my blood on his lips. I wanted more. I wanted with my whole body to keep going. To explore him more.

Pulling back from him, I gaped. *Shit!* The fog lifted slightly and I remembered where I was. I remember why I didn't want this here.

His eyes were their normal color, but there was so much need boiling just under the surface of his skin that, for the first time I could recall, he was warm to the touch. He reached up and brushed my bottom lip with his thumb.

I heard a giggle and clapping coming from behind me. Standing up, I smoothed my dress down and faced the hysterical vampire. I slowly walked back to my chair. I couldn't help the blush that spread across my cheeks. I hated that she saw me lose control like I had.

"Oh, Cannon. Such self-restraint. Your thoughts…" She closed her eyes and her pink tongue slipped out, tasting her lips. *Was that a shudder that passed through her?* "They were so vivid. The things you wanted to do to her. Mmmm. Shall I tell her?" There was an edge to her tone.

Before Cannon had a chance to respond, the door flew open. God bless Polo. He billowed into the room, clearing some of the built-up hormones and replacing it with cool fresh air. *Saved by the bell.*

"Oh, Polo, you have the worst timing. Poop on you!" Merriam scolded the confused vampire.

It didn't take a rocket scientist to see that something had happened. And clearly Polo could sense it. His eyes narrowed on Cannon as he walked over to Merriam and placed a large book in front of her. He then stood behind her and rested a firm hand upon her shoulder. All while never taking his gaze off Cannon.

Cannon, however, was looking well at me, his expression completely unreadable. I knew he wanted to talk or explain but this just wasn't the place or time.

"Leave." She spoke the word so softly I wasn't sure I really even heard her. There was danger there. Polo went rigid. My gaze flicked from him to her. He didn't move. Now, from everything I'd seen, this bitch wasn't one to be fucked with on any level and here was one of her peons defying her. Where was the popcorn when I needed it?

Her eyes flicked red just before Polo went flying across the small room. I, acting on instinct, pulsed my mental power. I was able to stop him from hitting the wall with only a few inches to spare. I had no idea why I'd acted, chalking it up to human stupidity. Hitting a wall wouldn't have killed him. I knew that. I guess I just didn't want him to get hurt.

Merriam's attention was well and truly on me. Her lips curled upward at the corners. Her eyes pinched slightly in a smile that never seemed to be reflected in the pale orbs.

"Pick him up again," she ordered.

"Um, what?" What the hell was she trying?

"Polo, leave. Call in Sarra." He scrambled to his feet and fled the room with haste.

Not a minute later did a small, fair vampire walk in. She looked as though she couldn't be more than eighteen. She matched my size nearly perfectly. Her delicate features were set off in a halo of bright-red hair that seemed to fan out in small waves of fire.

"Yes, ma'am?" Her voice was small and unsure. Of

the vampires I'd seen, she looked to be the shyest and most unsure. *Is she new? Possibly.*

"Addison. This is Sarra. She's small and pretty like you. You seem to want to play in this big bad game. So, now here is your chance."

I looked to Cannon, who was eyeing Merriam. Clearly he was just as confused as I was.

"Pick her up and throw her in to that wall." She pointed to the same wall that Polo had come within inches of hitting. "Do it or I'll take her head."

The petite vampire looked from me to her master. Any color that had been in her face all but drained. Was she serious? I blinked at her in confusion.

"Mas-" Her voice was cut off by a gabbled mess of sound. Her tiny hands grasped at some invisible force around her throat.

I pulsed my power, hoping to pick the small creature up and toss her. She didn't budge. I kept trying. Her eyes bore a hole through me, begging me to help her. I kept attempting to pick her up but just when I thought I had a hold of her, she would slip through my fingers. I switched my attention to Merriam and tried to use something to stop her, but she was just as slippery as Sarra.

"Stop!" I screamed.

Merriam's cold gaze locked on me. In a tone that matched her stony face, she said, "If you can't play with the adults, then you need to sit at the kiddy table."

I ran toward Sarra. I didn't know her. I didn't know why saving her meant so much to me, but it did. I pushed with everything I had and finally got ahold of her with my mental grip. I tossed her to the wall. Just before she hit it, I heard her garbled screams stop and a thud of her head hitting the floor.

Her headless body flopped like a dead fish against the wall before it fell awkwardly to the ground. Blood pooled around the crumpled form. Her head lay on the floor just beside her lifeless body. The cottony hair that seemed so full of life lay caked in blood.

My eyes burned with unshed tears.

"Why?" My voice was rough and tight. I'd done as she asked and she'd killed her anyway.

She shrugged. "You didn't do it fast enough."

I bit my tongue until I tasted blood.

Standing up, I brushed off my dress and walked to the door. I was done. I'd find some other way to find Lachlan and figure out how to deal with whatever baddy had him.

"Sit down!" Cannon's voice echoed off the walls of the small room, filling it with his commanding presence. I paused and turned, crossing my arms over my chest.

"Enough stalling. Enough games. Merriam, you've manipulated the situation enough and I'm running out of patience!" Cannon was snarling. Clearly he was done with her shit, too.

"Cannon, have you grown a backbone while I've been away?" Her tone was snide and condescending.

"Considering I've had to lead our people and pick up all of your slack, I've done what had to be done."

"Watch how you speak to me, Cannon, you might end up like poor Sarra."

He stood up and leaned down until he was a mere inch from her face. "You want a war. Then war it will be." He stood up and our eyes met. He too was done. When he reached me he drew his hand to my face and ran a thumb across my cheek. Oddly this above everything else that had happened rocked me to my core.

"A Litch," Merriam's voice called from behind us.

Cannon stiffened. Our eyes met. I saw what I would have considered to be fear flash across his stony features.

"Merriam, they are myth."

I turned and faced her fully.

"Well, you wanted to know what it was you were

dealing with and that's what it is. A Litch. A being that is immortal."

The silence stretched between us.

"If it's immortal, how the hell do we kill it?" I asked.

"To become immortal, the being had to rid itself of its soul. Something that was once human is now … warped. Strength like you've never seen. But, when the soul was separated, he had to keep it whole but in something, because ridding the soul completely would kill him. So, find wherever he's keeping the object that contains his soul and destroy it."

"Why does that seem too simple?" I asked.

Her face went deadly serious. "He likely carries it with him. The one I helped defeat did, anyway. The object could be anything. But, it will likely be a stone. Something easy enough to hide yet durable."

"Okay, so we just need to get close to him?" Cannon asked.

"By this time he's consumed so many lives that his power has grown to unspeakable levels. Also, not having one's soul in your body can make a being go quite mad," she informed us.

I thought it quite ironic that she was telling us this being would be so mad yet here she was, a few steaks short of a cow herself.

"Well, how exactly are we supposed to kill him if he's immortal, hella strong, and crazy as fuck?"

She ripped out a few pages from her book and stood up. She walked over to Cannon and stuffed the pages into his pants and gave me a wicked smile.

"Why, darling, how are you supposed to kill who?" she asked with a completely dazed tone.

"No one. Thank you, Merriam. We will see ourselves out," Cannon intoned as he turned to the door. We walked through. Polo met us and walked us to the front of the house. Behind me, I heard Merriam's frantic words.

"Oh gosh, Sarra! Who killed her?"

"You did, ma'am," I heard a voice reply.

"Oh? I did? What a shame. She was a great lay. Crap," were the last words I caught before Cannon, Polo, and I stepped outside. I shook my head. Merriam was batshit crazy. And I had no idea what the hell we were dealing with.

"Thank you," Polo whispered, not meeting my eyes.

Pausing, I spat, "For what? For allowing someone to die who wasn't you? For being the reason Sarra is dead? Yeah, you're so fucking welcome." I gritted my teeth. I would have been fine had he been the one to die. Not someone who had nothing to do with anything.

I continued forward without waiting for a response from him. I was beyond caring. Cannon's car was already running and waiting. He opened the door and I slid in. Cannon slid next me and shut the door. He met my eyes.

"So, that was…" I didn't know how to classify what just occurred.

"A clusterfuck?" Cannon finished.

"Yeah. Pretty much," I replied, leaning back on the seat and moving my attention to the passing scenery. I had a sudden thought. "What do the pages she so lovingly stuffed down your pants say?" Not that I was jealous. I wasn't.

Rolling his eyes, he reached in and grabbed them. He laughed and threw the papers at me. I unwrinkled them and eyed the writing.

How to kill the Litch:

Don't.

Well, that's helpful. I balled up the note and tossed it somewhere in the backseat of the car.

"Why do I have a distinct feeling that it's about to get a whole lot worse?"

Cannon didn't say anything. He didn't have to. I knew just how much deep shit we were in. A whole shit fuck ton. *Wonderful.*

Chapter Sixteen

Cannon had been nearly and completely silent on the way back to the hotel. The only words he spoke to me were a garbled mess telling me to get my shit together.

Merriam hadn't been a complete loss. We had an idea of what we were dealing with and how to deal with it, in theory anyway. Now, we just had to find it. Though I got the sense that this Litch we were dealing with was a complete monster that was nearly impossible to kill, and the one thing that could kill it was nearly impossible to find. In other words, we were screwed so hard we had better pray that someone took mercy on us and provided lube.

"Cannon?" I asked quietly. The whole damn trip back to Atlanta he'd completely given me the silent treatment and frankly I was so damn over it.

"What?!" he snapped back. I had no idea what crawled up his ass and died, but he'd better eradicate it, or I'd shove him onto the pavement quick, fast, and in a hurry.

"Cannon, I say this with all of my heart." I paused and looked him in the eyes. "How deeply embedded is the stick that's found its way up your ass?" Now, I know I could have been kinder and less crass, but hey that's not really my style.

"Addison…" He drifted off, looking as though he had to fight some kind of emotion. Then he did something that caught me completely off-guard. His lips quirked up into a brief smile and then he completely lost it. His guffaws of laughter filled the small space, making it impossible to do anything other than laugh with him.

"Leave it to you to talk to me in a way that most people would be dead for," he commented around a genuine smile. Had my heart sped up at seeing his features alight with that show of humanity? *No. Well, maybe. Crapcakes.*

"Cannon, how are we going to do this?" I asked, completely changing the mood in the car.

"Addison…" He was interrupted by the buzzing of his cell phone. I rolled my eyes in annoyance and gestured for him to answer the damn thing. As I was trying to shamelessly listen in on his conversation, my phone rang. I wrestled it from my pocket after a few rings and I managed to win the tug of war. I looked at the screen. It was Darryl's cell. I frowned. He never called me this late.

"Hello?" I said tentatively.

I heard something I couldn't quite make out. It was a number of voices. Three or four men maybe.

"Hello? Darryl? Did you butt-dial me?" Still no response. Just more talking that was just far enough away that I couldn't make out what was being said. Then I heard a scream of pain. A chill ran down my spine and cold fear washed completely over me. There were laughs that followed. A movie. He was watching a movie. He had to be.

"Darryl?! Please," I begged.

The screams continued. At first I had no idea if I was hearing a male or female but the person's blood-curdling screams turned to bellows that could only be from a man. I prayed this was some sick play I was hearing, but I knew it was real. My mouth went dry and a lump formed in my throat. My eyes locked with Cannon, who seemed to mirror my feelings.

Now more sounds were coming across the speaker. I could hear flesh being hit with something. I could hear grunts of pain. My eyes burned with unshed tears. I couldn't fight them. The hot liquid seemed to slowly sear my skin raw as they traced down my cheeks.

"Please, Darryl. I'm begging you," I whispered. I was only met with more sounds of pain.

Cannon's call had since ended. He reached over and pulled the phone from my hand and hit the speaker button.

Then I heard it. A distant voice. Maybe it sounded distant because my heart was beating so loudly it nearly drowned everything out.

"Addy, oh Addy. Little bird." The voice was guttural and harsh but he sang my name in a singsong way. My heart all but stopped.

"Who is this?" My voice quaked with fear but I really didn't care.

"Addy-son! Oh, little bird. I have a few things you may want!" Still in that singsong tone, he hissed the word *things*.

There is something so familiar about this voice, if I could only put my finger on it.

"I-I-" I swallowed, hoping to calm my thoughts. I needed to ask the right questions. I wasn't sure how long I had or if I'd get this chance again.

"I'd like to get them back. How should I go about doing that?" My throat was nearly closing under the stress.

"Well, you must follow the pebbles that glow in the

moonlight," the voice rasped. I heard more shouts of pain and more sounds of impacts.

I jerked back at that. Glowing pebbles? How had he known that? I remember being told the story of Hansel and Gretel when I was very little. My mother told it to me. She said she never understood why people told it with breadcrumbs because birds would, as she said, "eat that shit right up." So, instead, she said they were pebbles that glowed in the moonlight.

Swallowing, doing my best to pull my emotions in, I asked, "I haven't seen the pebbles. Where are they?"

"Ask the vampire with you."

I met Cannon's eyes. That's when I saw it. He was hiding something.

"I'll be here when you're ready. But they might not be. How many do I need to take, Addison?" His voice was growing angrier as he spoke, the words becoming harsher.

"Please let me talk with them," I begged. But the phone clicked and the screen went black.

I looked at the deep black pools of Cannon's eyes, unable to speak the thousand questions. His features were made of stone. Completely unreadable. And that only pissed me off.

"What-"

"Let me explain-"

We spoke at the same time.

Putting my hand up to stop him from going on any further, I spoke my next words with as much force as I could manage, "I swear, if you've been hiding things from me, Cannon…" I didn't really know what I'd do.

"Addison." He reached for my hand but I pulled back. I was not in the mood to be touched. I was in the mood for truthful communication, for him to be honest with me for once.

"Listen. I knew that someone had been sending you things. I had a feeling it was connected. I'd been looking into it. Then the book went missing. The same name kept popping up, A. Pebble. I have no idea who or what that is. But, I knew I'd seen the name before. The man who did the renovations on the dojo. I just learned about that connection before we left for Chicago."

My breath left me with a whoosh.

"You knew? You knew that Darryl was in danger and you did nothing?" I was completely tossed off balance.

"No, I know what he means to you. I had some people watching Darryl. I had them making sure no one bothered him."

"I guess that didn't fucking work, did it?" I was screaming and my vision was blurring with yet more acidic tears. They were threatening to burn me from the inside out.

"Addison. Damnit. I thought I had it under control. But I got a phone call, just now. The two I had watching him were ripped apart," he explained through gritted teeth.

"Cannon. You didn't think to tell me or Darryl? Like you just didn't think that was a good idea?" I spat.

"I didn't want you to tip them off, and I didn't want you to do something stupid."

I just blinked at him, dumbfounded. I'd never wanted to hit someone as much as I did in that moment. *I may have a tendency to rush into situations, but I don't think I'm a risk. Am I? God, maybe he was right not to tell me.*

"I do not regret any of this." His tone was so smug and detached.

I'm not human. The words he'd told me a million times seemed to echo in my mind over and over again. He gave yet another reminder that the face he wore to appear civilized was nothing more than paint.

The rest of the ride was spent in silence. I slept some, glared at him some, cried some, and realized just how lost I was. There was no way I could do this on my own, nor did I want to do this with him. I was in this never-ending loop of bullshit.

About four-thousand hours later, we pulled up to my apartment. As I got out of the car that had grown far too stuffy, I felt Cannon's iron grip circle my wrist.

I sighed. Speaking at that moment would have been a really bad idea. I would have likely told him to go stuff his cock in a blender.

"Addison, I want you to go get a few things and come back to my home with me."

Was he kidding? I raised an eyebrow at him and I couldn't stop myself from laughing at him.

"Cannon," I tried to get the words out between sobs of laughter. "Really? Have you lost your mind?"

I tried to pull my arm from his hold, but he only squeezed tighter as he slid out of the car. He nearly pulled me to the door. Shoving his other hand in my pocket, he fished around for something. *Oh hell no.* He pulled out my keys and opened the door, then dragged me up the stairs and jammed the key into the lock so hard I thought it had to have broken in the process.

"Cann-uff." He threw me in to my own fucking apartment.

Slamming the door behind him, he glared down at

me. I looked back up at him and put my hands on my hips. Real presence of power, I know.

"Listen here, you piece of shit ass-munching fuck face, I have no idea how, but I'm doing this without you."

"Shut up."

I rocked back as though he'd hit me. My eyes widened.

"Addison, I don't regret anything because it kept you safe."

"You're responsible for anything that happens to Darryl." My voice was low and controlled. Something I did not think I was capable of.

"Don't you think I know this? Damnit, Addison! I want to not care. I want be the ruthless bastard I was before you came into my life!" He was yelling at me and I couldn't understand why he was so upset. I was the one who should be upset.

"Why are you so pissed at me? And fucking hell, you need to learn how to speak to me! Stop yelling at me and ordering me around!" Great, now I was yelling.

He grabbed my hand and jammed it on his chest. I could feel the coolness of his skin seep through to my hand.

"Feel it! This lay dead in my chest for so long. And

every single day spent with you the damn thing beats stronger. I hate it because you're causing me to feel. I …" He paused, trying to find the right word, or so I assumed. "I worry about what you'll think of me. I worry about how things make you feel. I've been a monster for so long that I had become numb to feeling anything."

"Cannon, I…" I trailed off, not knowing what to say to him.

"I wanted to be hard and not care who I destroyed in the way of what I wanted. But now I don't think I can do that. God-damnit, Addison. I want to kill you."

I took a step back. Silly thing to do with a predator, but it was instinct. Especially when someone says they want to kill you.

"I want to kill you. But, it would ruin me to lose you. Yet, it's ruining me to have you." He ran a hand through his hair, causing the nearly black locks to fall free from the binding at his neck.

"You should have told me," I whispered, unable to meet his eyes. I didn't want to see his expression, because if it matched the desperation laced in his voice, I wasn't sure I could resist throwing my arms around him.

"I should have told Darryl. I made a mistake that

hurt you and him." His voice cracked, causing me to look up at him. I nearly staggered back at the pain reflecting back at me.

I wanted to hate him. I wanted to slap him in the face. I wanted him to be smug and the same bastard I knew. But he wasn't and I couldn't.

"What do we do now?" I asked, not really knowing anything anymore. I felt as though the rug had well and truly been pulled out from beneath me, shoved into a rocket launcher, and shot to kingdom come.

"I'm asking for you to come back with me. Not telling or ordering. From there, I'll explain everything that's been gathered." His face shifted from something readable to stone in the blink of an eye.

"And if I don't?" I asked the question mainly to see what he would do.

His jaw clenched and I thought I could hear him swallow whatever his first reaction was.

"Then I'll call my people, have them bring everything here. And I'll stay here." My eyes widened at his response. I did not want twenty of his closest vampires in my home.

"Okay, I'll get more clothes."

He turned to leave.

"Oh, and Cannon?"

Pausing with his hand on the knob, he turned to face me.

"I still hold you one-hundred percent responsible for anything and everything that happens to Darryl."

"I would expect nothing less." An emotion flashed across his face as he stepped out of the doorway. It happened so fast I very nearly missed it. It was resignation. It was that moment I began to hope? Think? Wonder? If maybe, he was right. Maybe, just maybe, he was feeling.

"Hello?" I croaked, hoping I'd actually turned the damn phone on.

What the hell time is it? I had to blink away the fog that covered my eyes. I was surrounded in the warm sleepy haze. And frankly, I wasn't all interested in making a coherent thought, much less holding a conversation on the phone.

"Um, Ms. Addison?" The voice was familiar. It was small and distant.

"Who is this? And do you know what time it is?" I snapped. I pulled the phone away from my ear and the screen lit up, blinding me for a second. *Damnit.* I blinked rapidly until the time came into focus. 3:12 a.m. *Oh for fuck's sake, someone better be dead.* Then, like a rubber band, my thoughts snapped into focus.

"It's me. Erica. I-I'm sorry it's late." She hiccupped. Clearly upset, she added a sniffle. "But I didn't know who else to call."

"No, it's okay, honey. I'm sorry I snapped. What's wrong?" I calmed my voice and sat up in the plush bed. Cannon said I was to sleep in his room. Well, not with him in it, thank God.

"It's my dad. He's been on the phone with the people he works with and, and…" She began sobbing so softly that my heart nearly exploded. "He's taking me somewhere tomorrow. To fix me. I tried to call my mom, but she's out partying or something. I-I-I don't know what to do!" Her words were so quiet and muffled that I had to strain to hear her. *Shit!* I had no idea what to do! I had no legal right to go take her. I tried to think of something but nothing came up. *What good is having these abilities if I can never seem to help or protect anyone?*

I looked up to see Cannon standing in the doorway. He was backlit, so he was only a dark silhouette. I looked at him, begging him to tell me the right thing to do.

"Erica, honey. What's your mom's number?"

She rattled of the number and I quickly jotted it down in the notepad on my phone.

"Erica, I'm going to try everything I can."

"Please come get me. You promised it would all be okay! You swore it!" Her little words were each a pin-prick in my heart, leaving my chest feeling as though it were on fire.

"I know, honey. I'm doing everything I can. But if I came and got you, I would get arrested for kidnapping. Please hold tight. I'm going to call your mom."

The line went dead. I pulled the phone away from my ear to see my home screen flashing. I threw the phone as hard as I could. I hadn't meant to throw it at Cannon, but he snatched it up with one hand before it met its untimely death against a wall. Thank God he had. I needed to stop reacting and start thinking.

"If you're quite done, would you care to talk about it?" he asked, walking toward me.

"What good is it?!" I yelled in utter frustration.

"What good is what?"

"Having these useless abilities. Getting my life together. None of it matters. I keep making mistakes. I can't even protect the people that I love. What the fuck is the point of any of this!?" I knew I was being over-dramatic, but for real, there was only so much until I snapped.

We both sat there in silence for several moments. I held my hand out and he placed my phone in it.

I quickly dialed Erica's mother's number, only to be met with her voicemail. I left a message asking her to call me as soon as possible, that her daughter was in trouble.

I hung up the phone and met Cannon's eyes.

"What do I do?" I asked, hoping he would know just how to fix this mess.

He frowned. "Addison, you know I can't help. If I could-"

"No, you wouldn't," I said, cutting off the lie I knew he was about to say. He wouldn't help unless it benefited him in some way.

"No, I likely wouldn't. But, Addison, we don't have time for this." His tone was so firm. I couldn't give two shits just how hard this vampire was.

"No. I will not let that little girl just be handed over to CAP. I swore to her she would be okay. I promised her, Cannon. I will not let her sink without at least trying to save her."

His eyes widened at the mention of CAP.

"Addison, CAP owns a lot of people in this town. They are the most powerful nonprofit hate group I've ever had the displeasure of dealing with."

I got up and walked to the pile of clothes that lay on the ground. I began putting them on.

"What are you doing?" he asked, eyeing me warily.

"Holding up my end of a promise. I don't know how but I'm going to go get her." I fumbled with my button on my jeans. Cannon's hands slipped over mine. His brief touch seemed to calm me slightly. I looked up and met his eyes.

"I can't get involved in this. But, I won't stop you. Just come back. We have bigger things to deal with." His other hand grasped my chin lightly.

Before I could protest, he kissed me, hard and desperate. His lips felt cool to my heated skin. He'd kissed me so many times and each time it felt different. This one, this one felt as though his need would overtake me and steal my very breath from my body. Who needed to breathe anyway, right?

His tongue slid into my needing mouth. It all suddenly crashed on me. His words echoed in my mind. "*What do you want*?" Right now, the answer was so simple it was nearing primal. I wanted him. I hated myself for wanting him so badly.

For the first time in all of our interactions, I kissed him back with all of the raw need I felt built up in my whole being. He moaned at the change. I opened to him fully. His tongue flicked mine and I met him lap for lap. I pulled him closer. I somehow didn't know how to go on without doing this, without expressing my want for him.

He ripped his mouth from mine, leaving me panting and aching for his touch. My eyes caught his. The man looking back at me looked animalistic and savage. His eyes were beyond black, if that was even possible. But I wasn't afraid; if anything I was drawn deeper into the rabbit hole.

"Leave," he snarled.

I stared at him. I was still panting in huge gulps of air, so maybe I hadn't heard him correctly.

"Wha-what?"

"You have someplace to be. This," he motioned between us, "will likely take more time than you have."

I didn't understand at first. I had someplace to be? *OH! Crap, Erica!* I stepped to the side and grabbed my clothes. I threw them on as I made my way to the front door.

"Addison." I had no idea how, but every time he called my name it caused everything inside of me to stop even for just that moment. I turned slightly, acknowledging him without speaking.

"We've gone too far. I won't let you go back now." The timbre of his tone was so low it shook the very foundation I was standing on.

"I wouldn't if I could," I said, walking out the door. It wasn't until I heard the soft click behind me that I realized it was true. There was no turning back. He'd taken up a part of my heart despite any fight I put up. I couldn't stop a small smile from spreading across my face, even if this was a bad idea.

Chapter Seventeen

Erica's house was about thirty minutes outside of Atlanta. Cannon had one of his drivers take me. I couldn't really protest, as when I left the building, the car was waiting and I didn't want to be rude, despite the fact that it would be faster to run.

The driver, however, was one I'd not seen before. I always made it a practice to get to know the people around me. I thought it only polite.

"Hey there, I'm Addison. What's your name?" I asked, hoping to kill some of the time on the drive.

The tall lanky man had sandy-blond hair and rich brown eyes. He had a scar that ran from his hairline down the side of his face, curving around his right eye down past his chin, stopping at his neck.

"Simon." His tone was gruff. His eyes flicked to me and rolled. Clearly he either did not like driving or he didn't like driving me. Either way he seemed to be annoyed.

I eyed his scar. I couldn't help but wonder what

happened. How he could have possibly gotten it. I wanted to ask but really didn't want to be rude about it.

His eyes flicked to mine and I quickly looked away. Feeling like a kid whose hand had been caught in the cookie jar, I forced my eyes to the rapidly passing objects.

He sighed, "Just ask."

I felt like an ass because I'm sure everyone asked. "How?"

"Cannon."

I wanted to be surprised. I wanted to have the first thing to come to mind be, "Oh my gosh, he would never!" But, sadly, it didn't.

He laughed a low, smooth laugh.

"You don't look surprised."

"I'm not."

I didn't care about the why of it. I didn't need to know. Would it really matter in the end? Cannon was Cannon. He would always have a hard, unforgiving edge to him. He would always cut when he meant to caress. That, in the end, was who he was.

The rest of the ride was spent in long, drawn-out silence.

I glanced at the clock just as we pulled in front of Erica's house. It read 4:53 a.m. I had no idea what in the hell I would accomplish by being here but I had to try.

Getting out of the car, I was so conflicted and distracted that I nearly tripped over my feet.

"Oh, she who is full of grace, I'll wait here," I heard Simon say behind me.

I rolled my eyes and scoffed in return.

The bright-red door seemed daunting sitting in front of me like some kind of beacon.

Knocking on the wooden door, I had to stop myself from darting around the bushes. I really did not want to have this talk with Kyle.

The once-dark house sprang to life with upstairs lights turning on and footsteps coming ever closer. Kyle, who was oddly fully dressed, swung the door wide. He also didn't look shocked to see me.

I stood there just blinking at him. Had he been awakened by Erica's call? Had he known I'd come by?

"Um," was all I could say.

He stepped to the side, inviting me in. I glanced behind me and saw Simon's silhouette in the driver's seat. I could hear little alarm bells going off. Something wasn't right. I stepped in anyway.

Kyle locked the door before turning to face me.

"Hey, um, Kyle, I um…" My voice drifted off, hearing muffled cries coming from just up the stairs.

EMILY CYR

My eyes followed the pale-cream carpeted stairs. Past the black-and-white family photos lovingly hung along the wall to the door with *Kung-Fu Panda* stickers littered across it. I could just barely make out what was being said.

"I'm so sorry. They made me. I'm sorry." I didn't understand the context until I trained my eyes on the person to the right of me. The fact that he'd moved from behind hadn't alarmed me; however, the fact that he stood there with a gun pointed at me did.

I took an instinctive step back. His eyes bored into mine with an intensity and hatred I'd never seen from him before.

"Hell, Kyle! Your daughter's in the house. What are you thinking?!" I nearly yelled. I could kick his arm, breaking the damn thing, but he could possibly squeeze off a shot before I could stop him, and with Erica in the house I wasn't willing to risk that. The space was a little small for me to go all Speedy Gonzales on him, so that option was out. My telekinetic ability could work, but again, I would surely hate to have it go on the fritz as it tended to do. The lifeless vampire laying in a pool of her own blood because of my inaction flashed in my mind. I couldn't make that mistake again. I had to diffuse this situation in another way and be smart about it.

His jaw clenched and a fine sweat broke out over his brow. His eyes weren't quite focused. He didn't want to be doing this either. *What the hell is going on?*

"Addison, please walk to the kitchen." His voice shook.

"Kyle, I've never been here. So, I don't know where it is," I commented calmly. The last thing I wanted to do was piss off someone with a gun who already seemed to be upset. No need to make his trigger finger suddenly slip.

His eyes widened. "Oh, um, down the hall behind you then off to the left." His hands were now visibly shaking.

"Kyle, what kind of trouble are you in? I can he-"

"S-s-shut up! Just walk!" he yelled, cutting me off.

I turned and made my way through the house to the kitchen. I was about halfway to what I assumed was the kitchen from the amount of light that was spilling onto the hallway when I heard the faint murmuring of voices. I couldn't tell by sound alone how many there were, but it was more than two. I glanced over my shoulder to Kyle. He clearly had some major doubts about what he was doing. I stopped and turned to face him fully.

Lowering my voice, I rushed the words, "I don't

• 2 3 0 •

know what you got yourself and Erica into, but I can help. You don't have to do this."

He shook his head, saying, "No one can help. This is what's best."

I didn't believe for one second that he bought what he was saying, not for one moment.

Turning from him, I continued to walk toward the voices. I had no idea what this was all about, but it seemed like I wouldn't be given much of a choice but to find out.

I rounded the corner to find myself face to face with three people. Two men and one woman. None of whom I could ever recall meeting or even seeing before.

"Hello, Addison. I'm sure all of this must be confusing but please have a seat so we can talk," the portly white man with the awful comb-over said, gesturing to an open kitchen seat.

"If you wanted to talk to me, you should have thought about not asking Kyle here to use his daughter to get me here and then have him draw a goddamn gun on me. You ass waffles clearly know who I am. I have no idea who any of you are, and to be honest, I think I'd rather get a tit ripped off by a rabid penguin than get the chance." I refused to be polite at this point.

I wouldn't risk anyone's safety by freaking out on these morons.

"I understand how all of this looks, but Kyle assured us that if we tried to meet with you in other ways, you would simply run," the sharply dressed woman interjected.

I looked at Kyle and scoffed, "Well, Kyle doesn't know his head from his balls. So, here's the deal. You have ten minutes. I can easily get upstairs, get Erica, and be halfway to my car before you could scratch your asses. I'm simply being polite." They all looked at each other as though I'd just dropped a bomb of information.

"Ms. Fitzpatrick. Please, all we want to do is talk," the woman pleaded.

"You have a funny way of expressing that." I eyed all of them and turned to push past Kyle. I was so over this bullshit.

"Please, Addison," Kyle begged, placing the gun on a nearby counter.

I glared at him.

"You have not given me one reason to stay. You've only given me ones to leave," I spat at him. Just as I pushed past him, I heard the woman say two words. The only two words that could have ever been said that would physically prevent me from moving another step.

"Darryl Monroe."

It wouldn't have mattered if she said more. All I could hear was the rush of blood surging to my heart as the wild muscle in my chest threatened to beat its way out of me. I tried to inhale even half a breath but only managed to swallow back every emotion that seemed to have rushed to the surface.

"What does her boss have to-"

"Shut up," I whispered. I focused on a photo hanging on the wall just opposite me. It was of Erica when she was just a baby. She looked to be asleep, yet she was smiling. I wondered if I ever had dreams like that? So innocent they would make me smile. Or if I'd been born with nightmares. I closed my eyes. I had to center myself. *I may never get this chance again; I will not fuck this up by being me.* This was more important than me, maybe I was learning to control my impulses.

Slowly, I turned around to face the three strangers and Kyle. I flicked my eyes to him. He looked confused as he eyed the intruders sitting so smugly in his kitchen.

Each of them was dressed as though they were going to a damn business meeting. But I couldn't care less. I clenched my hands into fists and could feel the blood draining from my face.

"Now, that we have your attention," the once-silent man spoke with a voice that had a very southern twang. He would have been somewhat attractive, had he not been part of this mess. He looked to be in his early forties with salt-and-pepper hair that was cut close on the sides and left longer on the top. He had a matching beard that somehow caused his piercing blue eyes to spark. "Please, have a seat." He gestured just as the man before him had done. I bit the inside of my cheek to keep from saying anything, feeling the warm taste of iron before my ass hit the chair. I tried not to look indignant, but I'm sure I did.

"Damien. What the hell-" Kyle tried, but was stopped by the silver-haired man's words.

"Ms. Fitzpatrick. My name is Damien. This is Seraphina," he motioned to the brown-haired woman to his right, "and that is Rodrick." He again indicated the plump man who had first spoken to me.

"We are representatives from CAP," Damien explained.

This wasn't something that caught me off-guard, I'd assumed they were in CAP. However, the mention of Darryl's name had completely blindsided me.

"Okay, and I'm a pusher. My boss, however, is not. So, please explain to me why I'm here and why his name would come out of your mouths." My words dripped so heavily with disdain that I'd be surprised if there weren't a puddle on the floor.

"Well, Ms. Fitzpatrick. We have a little issue," Seraphina spoke. Her words held a hint of amusement. If I already hadn't disliked her I'd really hate the bitch for that damn glint in her eyes.

"Okay. And, that would be?" I hedged.

"To put it simply, you." She was actually able to say that last bit without that chip on her shoulder falling off.

"You see, our benefactor. You know what that is, don't you?" She spoke the words as though she were speaking to a dimwitted child. I again bit the inside of my cheek to stop myself from shoving my foot so far up this woman's ass that she would be tasting rubber for a month.

"The man who pumps our organization full of money, wants to study you."

Okay, so of all of the things that she could have said, that statement was so far out of left field I could only blink at her. How the fuck did any of them even know about me? I looked at Kyle. I'd kill him.

"Our organization is hell-bent on eradicating the pusher threat from the face of the Earth. But, to do so we need to stop it on a genetic level. We tried a few months back, but our lead geneticist was unfortunately killed."

Well, fuck me. Was this it? Was this the connection? But, damnit, it didn't make sense. Why would they try to turn pushers? I shook my head, trying to fully focus on her.

"Our benefactor has stated that if we could not get you to agree he would..." She swallowed. Her face paled before she was able to find her next words, "He would cease all support financially and otherwise."

"So, again I'll ask. Why mention Darryl?" I snarled through clenched teeth.

"Our benefactor gave us an address and time that he said you would be interested in. He informed us he knew where his pet was keeping Darryl." Damien replied.

Ah, there it was. Why would this "benefactor" know anything about this Litch or him having my friends? Was that what he meant by pet? Litch? The questions that kept popping up in my head were innumerable.

"Okay? Are you referring to the Litch?" I spoke the word as if it were a question, hoping to understand what they wanted.

"All we need is your word. Oh, and a sample of your blood. Our benefactor knows that you are the link to the destruction of your kind." He spat the word *kind* as though it were something disgusting. Though he didn't answer about the Litch and that made me question the involvement of the CAP at all.

"First, your benefactor. Why would he help me? And, you mentioned his pet. Do you mean the Litch?" I needed this answered.

"I would never think of what he was doing as helping you, but rather helping the CAP." *More like playing all sides for his own benefit.* "As far as his pet, well, I'll let you surmise what that means," Damien explained.

I didn't see as I had too many options. My guess was this mystery man had gotten the report Jack did on my blood and he wanted more. When Brent uploaded that virus, it had to have corrupted all of the files, including that one. Or at least I was guessing. The thought of Jack, the nut monster whom I had to cozy up to, to find out just what kind of drug he was concocting.

This money man had his hand in just about every pot, but I couldn't, for the life of me, figure out why. This connection to CAP seemed to be a little too, well, easy. But, bring Jack into the mix and this crazy shit with the Litch and it was just confusing as hell. The one thing I knew for sure was this money man was playing all angles, all sides for him and him alone. I highly doubted he cared one way or the other about CAP.

I did know one thing, this was a trap and would likely come back to bite me in the ass. I knew whatever he needed my blood for would not be good. But, if it led me to Lachlan and Darryl, then it had to be worth it.

"What is this address?" I had to ask. I couldn't just assume.

"Our benefactor said that it would lead you to the people you needed to save," Rodrick stated.

"Save? What does that mean?" Kyle's tone was frantic.

"Kyle, stay out of this," Seraphina snapped.

"No, you threatened my daughter and forced me to do this. What the hell is going on? I deserve to know."

"No. you don't," Damien intoned, standing up and pulling another gun out of his jacket pocket. Before I had time to register anything I heard a soft pop and Kyle fell to the floor. I lunged for Kyle.

"Now, Ms. Fitzpatrick, I would hate to inform our benefactor you were difficult to work with in this matter."

I only heard his words peripherally. I was hyper

focused on Kyle. He was moaning in pain and clutching his leg. I raked my eyes over him, trying to find the wound. Upper thigh on the outside. Looked like a through and through. I pressed on the wound and Kyle howled in pain.

Whipping my head to Damien, I hissed, "What the hell is wrong with you?! There is a child in this house!" What the fuck was he thinking?

"Ms. Fitzpatrick, I think we are done playing games here. If it were up to us we would execute every single one of you pushers. I can't do that. However, like I said before, we're done playing games. What's your answer?"

I gritted my teeth hard. Pulling Kyle's hand down to the wound, I pressed it firmly and stood.

"Fine. Whatever."

"Please, come sit here." Seraphina motioned to the kitchen chair directly across from her.

"Here, Kyle, hold pressure here. It's going to hurt like hell," I instructed as I got up and walked over to the table.

The woman opened up a small kit holding three vials and the necessary tools for a blood draw. She pulled the butterfly needle and connecting tube out then the small alcohol pads. I began making a fist and releasing it. She was taking for goddamned ever.

"For fuck's sake," I groused and grabbed the swab

from her hand. I rubbed it lower on my forearm, as the veins in the crook of my arm were complete shit.

"Hey, wait. I need it from your inner arm."

"Well too bad, sweetheart. Years of intravenous drug use have shot my veins to shit. So you get what you get." I glanced at Kyle. His face was paler than before. *Shit.* I didn't think he would die, but he needed medical attention.

The woman took in a shocked breath. I just rolled my eyes at her. I didn't need to explain myself to anyone, much less her.

Grabbing the needle, I slid it in. I had to stifle a small moan at the feeling. I nodded at her to connect the vials. In about a minute she had what they had come here for. Right now, I couldn't worry about why they wanted it. I had to help Kyle. Once I removed the tubing and such, I ran to him.

The three douche goblins got up and walked past me. Damian handed me one envelope. I dropped it on the floor. I desperately cared what was in that letter, but I had to help Kyle.

"We will show ourselves out," I heard a female voice echo down the hallway.

"Fuck faces," I whispered under my breath, kneeling back down to inspect Kyle.

Blood was pooling under him and his eyes were pinched. I placed my hands over his and applied yet more pressure. This was difficult while trying to stop my own puncture wound from bleeding out. He sucked in a breath and his eyes locked onto mine, but for only a moment.

"I need to call an ambulance," I muttered in a tone I knew was way too harsh, but damnit he'd drawn a fucking gun on me.

"Wait," he grumbled through clenched teeth.

I paused. I couldn't wait to hear what kind of bullshit he was about to spew.

"Please. Listen."

"Kyle, you need medical attention."

"Plea-"

"Daddy?"

I didn't take the time to think. I just ran and rushed her up the stairs to her bedroom, or what I assumed was her room.

"Honey-uff." She ran at me, grabbing me in a fierce hug.

"I'm so sorry. Daddy made me call you and say those things."

"Oh, honey, I know. Listen, I need you to make me a promise. I need you to stay here until I come get you okay?"

Her eyes sparkled with unshed tears. She was a smart kid. She knew something was wrong.

"You're not mad?" she whispered, unable to meet my eyes. Her shoulders were slumped and features drawn.

"Of course not," I comforted, cradling my hands around her tiny face.

I felt my fingers dampen under her heated skin. I wiped her tears with my thumbs. My throat tightened and my eyes burned with emotion. But, I only smiled.

"I need to go help your daddy. Please be a brave girl and stay here."

Closing her eyes, she nodded, causing yet more tears to spill. I turned and left the room for fear that her tears were contagious.

"Is she okay?" Kyle gritted.

"Yeah, she's shook up because of what you made her do. But, I don't think she saw this mess." I couldn't help but add the jab.

"They made me get you here. They told me they would take Erica and kill her."

None of this made any sense. I guess my confusion showed on my face because he continued.

"I called a friend, I thought he was a friend anyway, in the CAP and told them about you. Told him that maybe you weren't all bad. I didn't mention Erica because I was hoping to make a clean break." He shifted and sucked in a sharp breath. His jaw clenched and his face paled slightly.

"Kyle, please let me get some help. If you won't let me call an ambulance, let me go tell my driver and he can take you. You won't be of use to anyone if you bleed out on your kitchen floor." I wanted to hear everything, but I guess his life had to be a priority.

"Fine, but please know I didn't know what any of this was about. The three people that were here I'd never met. They asked me a number of questions about you. I thought maybe they'd found out about Erica but they really only cared about you. Like they'd been looking for you."

I didn't have time to think about this. I ran out to get Simon, finding him leaning against his car. Likely, he could see the panic on my face after the three butt plugs left because he didn't hesitate walking forward. He stopped short just outside the door. I glanced back at him questioningly. He raised his eyebrows at me and waited as though he were waiting for me to make some revelation.

Oh. Vampire. *He can't come in.*

"Please come in," I invited.

He shook his head as if I were about as stupid as they came.

"You don't call this place home. I need someone that lives here to invite me."

"Well, shit, I didn't know," I chided. "Kyle, tell Simon he can come in!" I yelled.

"Whatever, come in!" Kyle yelled back.

The tall man rolled his eyes and walked in without issue. He spotted Kyle and stopped.

"Why am I not surprised?" Simon asked smugly.

"Oh, shut up and get him to your car and to a hospital," I snapped as I bent down and picked up the envelope and shoved it into a pocket.

Simon helped Kyle up and proceeded to walk him to his car. Kyle's features were pinched in pain. I wouldn't have been a bit surprised had he cracked a tooth with how tightly he'd been clenching his jaw.

"Wait!" Kyle nearly yelled.

Both Simon and I paused.

"Please take Erica next door. To the Brown's. Promise me, Addison. Swear to me you'll make sure she's okay."

I nodded and assured him I would. Simon grumbled something about not getting blood all over his seats, but I ignored him.

I had to explain to Erica why I had blood all over my jeans. I glanced down to my arm. And apparently I'd have to explain my own bloody arm. She was upset, to say the least, but I was finally able to get her calm and over at the neighbor's house. Thank god they were too delirious from sleep to notice my red-covered pants.

I pulled Erica into a hug just before I left.

"I am so damn proud of you." I ran a hand over her head.

Kneeling down, I met her eyes.

"I love you, kid. I'll call you in the morning. Remember how special you are, okay?"

She nodded and threw her arms around me, squeezing me so tightly I didn't know if I could take in a breath. But it didn't matter, some things were worth losing your breath over.

"I will if you will," she whispered. I pulled back to look at her fully.

"Don't forget how special you are too," she reiterated. I nodded and left, no longer trying to hold back the tears. They fell for a reason; maybe I should let them.

Chapter Eighteen

Running back to Cannon's would be easy. Having to face him covered in blood would be a pain in the padded ass. So, I did what I always did. I avoided the situation. I headed to my place to just catch my breath.

This whole mess had just gotten incredibly complex. There was this money man, who seemed to have his finger in just about every pie. But why? It didn't make sense. I mean, he funded Jack, but I didn't believe he was a member of CAP. Unless the money man was using Jack for CAP's advancement without him knowing. That didn't feel right to me though.

And this man needing my blood? That seemed way too damn easy. Jack had said that I was the missing link, but I didn't take that to mean that my blood could be the key to getting rid of all of the pushers. This all seemed to be a puzzle with missing pieces. Or hell, maybe I was jamming pieces together that simply didn't fit.

I slowed as my apartment came into view. There were two shadowy figures looming on either side of the entrance to the small building. One impossibly tall and the other relatively short. I shook my head. I had no idea what these two morons wanted, but that didn't mean I couldn't mess with them.

I picked up my speed and ran to the shorter of the men. I snaked out a hand and caught his pants and pulled down swiftly, unable to stop the chuckle that slipped through my lips.

"Oh come on, Addison!" Rat groaned as he bent over to pull his pants back up.

Twinkie busted out in laughter. The big man couldn't seem to catch his breath. His arm wrapped around his middle and the other hand slapped the building. I couldn't stop my own laughter.

"Shut up, Twinkie!" Rat scolded the bigger man all while trying to shimmy his pants over his overly large hips.

"What are you guys doing here?" I directed my question to Twinkie, knowing Rat would be the one to answer me.

"The witch asked us to be here at this time to give you a note," Rat grumbled.

"Aww, and to think I thought it was because you

missed my pretty face." I rolled my eyes at Rat, who finally managed to pull his pants up.

"Not hardly," he scoffed.

"I think you're pretty, Addy," Twinkie coyly stated.

My cheeks warmed slightly as I glanced to the lumbering man.

"I think you're very handsome yourself, Twinkie." The tall man looked away sharply, but not before I could see his face flood with a pale-pink flush.

"If you two are done flirtin, we have a job to do," Rat insisted.

"Oh? And what is that?" I raised an eyebrow in his direction.

"Yeah, the witch asked us to deliver you a message," he stated proudly.

"Oh. Okay, well, what is it?" I asked, looking from him to Twinkie and back.

"Oh fuck, that woman rambles like a crazy person. She wrote it down. Twinkie! Give her the letter, you big oaf."

I turned fully to face Twinkie, who couldn't meet my eyes. He handed me a bright neon-pink envelope. I caught a scent of something sweet, like flowers and candy. I glanced down and rolled my eyes. The witch had scented stationary. I shouldn't be surprised.

"Wait, why are you covered in blood?" Rat asked, eyeing my pants.

"I just killed a man."

"Whatever. That's it. Let's go, Twink," Rat called as he turned to go down the street.

"Addy," Twinkie whispered as he walked by.

I looked up, trying to meet his eyes. Considering how short I was and how tall he was, that task was impossible. He leaned down to meet my gaze.

"Be careful. I thinkin sometin bad happenen to you." He really didn't talk a whole lot, so his words shook me. Then he did something I knew was special for him. He wrapped his large arms around me and squeezed me in a huge bear hug. I hugged him back. A moment later he was gone, leaving me wondering what the hell was going on.

I looked up at the small brick building. *Why am I here?* What I was running from no longer seemed that important. Without going in or sparing a second glance I turned and ran to Cannon's.

I wasn't even sure why I tried to tiptoe into the damn place. Cannon was like a freaking blood hound. I didn't even get to close the front door behind me before he was on me like white on rice. Well, if white gave rice the third degree about why it was covered in blood that clearly wasn't theirs.

"I tripped and fell?" I hedged, knowing there was no way in hell he would believe a single word I said. I guess he could pull the information out of my head, but he swore to me that he wouldn't do that. I had to believe that he was holding up that end of the deal.

Sighing, I explained what went down at Kyle's. I knew he knew some of it. I wasn't dumb enough to think Simon didn't call and tell him.

With only a grumble, he walked away. I mean, not a scolding, nothing. I followed behind him.

"What, you're not going to yell at me or tell me how stupid I am?" I questioned, hoping for some kind of reaction. Anything that would help me read how he was feeling. *Oh god, when did I start caring what Cannon Blackwood thought?* Maybe I was dying. Yup, that had to be it. That was the only explanation. Welp, it's been a great run world, but-

"Addison, you're rambling," he informed me, standing at the entrance of his room. *I am? Did I say any of that aloud?*

I paused, just now realizing he'd forgone his need for a shirt. His taut stomach was lean, but I was willing to bet if I were in need of a washboard his abs would

• 2 5 0 •

more than suffice. His jogging pants hung low on his hips, giving me a delicious glance of a dark trail that was leading to someplace I wasn't sure I should go. I licked my lips. I couldn't seem to stop the motion from happening.

"I'm not scolding you because you handled the situation in the way you saw fit," he explained. Had his tone darkened, lowering to that beautiful huskiness? No. It hadn't. Wait. His words hit me like a physical blow. I met his eyes.

"You mean you're not mad?" This really took me back. I mean, he was mad if someone dare farted in his general direction. He didn't say anything. Only a slow, warm laugh came from his lips. I flicked my eyes to his. They were their beautiful rich, deep dark color. The color that seemed to take over everything.

"It's hard to have a conversation with someone when all they seem to do is ogle your body." My eyes widened at his words. *Oh well, I guess I just got caught eyeing the cookie jar.* But, it's just such a pretty cookie jar.

He reached out and yanked me to him. My over-heated breasts pressed firmly to his cool skin. He was so cold I broke out in goose flesh over just about my whole body.

I contemplated telling him everything, telling him we had no time to waste. But, the truth was I was scared. I was scared of being with him. I was terrified of letting myself fall for him and ruining things with Lachlan. There would be no going back.

"There, there is a letter. The fuck nuts from the CAP," I said a little breathlessly. Standing so close to him like this sent a spike of desire right through me and settled between my legs, leaving a growing ache.

He shook his head at me in … disappointment? I couldn't tell, but just as fast as the emotion had been there it left.

Taking a step back he asked, "May I see it?"

Oh right. I reached in my pocket and grabbed it. I hoped I had the correct one because I really didn't want to tell him about the letter from Evie. Wait. If they had wanted my blood so badly they could have just gone to Cannon. I mean, money talks. No, he would never sell me out. I shook my head to get myself back in the game.

I opened the envelope. All it had was an address and time. My skin grew cold at the location. I knew immediately where this house was. I just couldn't figure out why.

"Addison?" Cannon asked. I blinked up at him. By the look on his face he'd been saying my name for some time.

I wanted to tell him. I wanted the words to jump out of my mouth without actually having to think about them. I wanted him to just know without me having to tell him anything.

This address was where the nightmares started. It wasn't where the worst of them were created, but they absolutely began there. I refused to cry or let this in any way send me back to that scared child I used to be.

Yet I couldn't seem to form the words.

"You know this address, don't you?" He whispered the question so low that had the room not been so quiet, I would have missed the words.

I nodded.

Taking a deep breath, the words fell from my lips as though it was the opening of a wound.

"It was a foster home. It was horrible there. I was just a child, but it was a place where I was in constant fear that I'd be beaten at every turn. I swore I'd never go back there. Just like I did with my aunt's home." But now I had to. I'd have to face the big bad demon as well as this monster. I couldn't speak anymore. I couldn't for fear of reliving every single childhood nightmare. I'd grown up and grown past that. I was an adult, but these memories threatened to take over and overwhelm every part of me. I utterly refused to be pulled down by this place, by these memories. I knew this A. Pebble and money man wanted this location to cause me pain. Pain can only break a person if they let it. I, for one, preferred to build on it.

I guess we need to go to this address.

"Why?" Cannon asked, grabbing the paper from my hand. His face hardened into its unreadable norm.

"Why what?" I blinked up at him, not really understanding his question.

"Why would they just hand over this information?" There it was. *Shit.*

"Um, I don't know." I could hear the lie in my own voice.

"Try again. I'll wait." He backed into the room until he bumped the bed and sat down. His eyebrows raised and there was a small smile tugging the corners of his mouth. He could just rifle through the shit in my head and take the information he wanted, but he was allowing me the time to give it to him willingly. Though, the white line forming along his jaw made me think that if I didn't, he would go dumpster diving for it.

I took a deep breath and then let it out slowly, explaining to him what this money man wanted. I told him I let them take a sample of my blood.

"Why do you always wait to tell me the important

information?" Cannon asked. I knew I'd heard that question before, but I pushed it aside and tried to focus on everything going on in that moment.

He flipped the letter in his hand over. There was writing on it I hadn't seen at first glance. His face went from unreadable to enraged in a moment. He flew to his feet, stormed over to the door and ripped the fucker off its hinges, then proceeded to throw the thing down the hallway as if it were nothing more than a napkin. Apparently, Cannon was having the equivalent of a Vampire hissy fit.

I heard footsteps rumbling down the hallway, followed by voices. I ignored them and walked over to the letter Cannon had dropped in his tantrum.

What could have been in a note that pissed him off so thoroughly? Flipping the paper over, I glared down at it.

There was an address with a time and date. On the back, there was a note:

Isn't it funny, for a vampire who could buy anything, you haven't been able to nail her yet? Sure you've had her blood, but soon so will I.

The game is on. Happy hunting.

What. The. Actual. Fuck? Whoever this guy was, he had a beef with Cannon and I was caught in the middle of it. Was any of this even about me? It seemed to be, but then it didn't. There were a thousand questions swirling around in my mind and it felt like I was being pulled under with no one to help me out.

I let the paper fall from my hand to the floor. I glanced up to see Cannon glaring at me. Oh fuck no. There was only so much a person could handle before they just snapped like a twig under a boot.

"What?" I snarled.

"You're going to just stand there and pretend you have no idea who this fucker is?" He stomped forward until he was about two feet away. I stood my ground. He was livid and he was taking it out on me. Well, I was done a long time ago being a punching bag. I was the one who does the punching now.

Taking a step to close the distance, I yelled, "No, I have no idea who this fuck twat is! So, vampire, back the hell up off of me and go eat a bag of dicks!"

His jaw clenched so hard I thought I heard his teeth crack. His eyes bore into me. But, hell no, I wasn't going to back down from this.

"Wait, do you know who this is? Is that why you suddenly have a gigantic stick up your ass?" I spat the question.

"No! I have no damn clue who this is. They clearly

know me and know details about us." He paused and grabbed my shoulders. "He knows things about you. Do you know just how much it scares me that I can't protect you? That there is something after you and they could use me to get to you? Do you understand how powerless that makes me feel?"

My breath left me in a whoosh because I understood. This vampire was powerful, yet he couldn't seem to protect the one thing he wanted. I had no idea what I needed anymore, but Cannon was right. This wasn't about that. It was purely about what I wanted and, right now, I wanted him. I felt deep inside of me that he cared. I could see the smallest flicker of hope inside of him. I prayed it wasn't wishful, stupid, misguided, seeing what I wanted to see, kind of thing.

I raised a hand, slipping it behind his head, running my fingers into his silky dark locks.

He groaned slightly. My heart was racing and my mind was screaming. I had no idea if this was the smart or right thing to do, but I wasn't sure I cared anymore. I pulled his face down to mine and crushed my lips to his. Somehow, through all of this, my feelings had softened to him, but my mind had muddled. But, right in that moment, I pushed everything aside and just acted.

His lips parted at the contact, letting me probe his mouth fully. He was not the type to give up control in any way, but right now he was letting me explore whatever this was.

His hands gripped my waist tightly, letting me know that his restraint was only a moment away from breaking.

I let my tongue slip into his mouth, where he met me lap for lap. What started as a cool kiss turned into something heated and near boiling.

His hands tightened on my hips and he ground himself against me. I could feel his erection hard against my belly. Pure need rocketed through me, leaving my knees weak and my restraint even weaker. His cool skin became heated under me. He didn't have a shirt on, so I let my hands trail over his firm and sculpted back. I wanted to dig my nails into the flesh, but resisted.

Every time a question of whether this was the right thing to do popped into my head, he chased it away with a lap of his tongue or a nip of his teeth.

God, what is he waiting for? Undress me already!

A low, deep laugh rumbled through his chest. I pulled away to see what was so damn funny.

"Addison." His tone was dark and low. God, that

alone sent a spike of need to settle right between my legs. "This needs to be your choice. I made mine a long time ago."

He was right, damn him. I stepped back and reached for the hem of my T-shirt. Slowly, I raised it, exposing my skin to the cold air. That brief contact with the air caused my skin to break out in goose flesh. Or at least I hoped it was the air. I pulled the cotton shirt over my head and tossed it to the floor, then met his eyes. They were locked on mine. And bless that vampire, he didn't so much as twitch for what I assume was fear that I would do the one thing I always did: run.

I reached behind my back and undid the clasp of my bra, letting the white lace fall to the floor along with the shirt. Cannon's eyes went from dark to all black. There was something so erotic about knowing how much just the sight of me turned him on. Knowing I caused him to feel that way caused my sex to throb so deliciously.

I reached for my pants and flicked the button open. Apparently, he'd had enough and charged me. Slamming me against the wall, his hands grabbed my wrists and pinned them above my head. With his free hand, he reached toward the hem of my pants. He buried his face in the crook of my neck and licked a slow, wet path along the soft oversensitive skin. I couldn't help but thrust my pelvis toward him, praying for friction of any kind.

He pulled the zipper down one painfully slow notch at a time. I was panting, trying desperately to fill my lungs with much-needed air. Finally, he tugged my jeans down and let them pool around my feet. I wiggled my feet free from the tangled denim. He groaned at the movement.

"Last chance, roadrunner," he half snarled, half hissed in my ear.

I said nothing. I just arched my bare chest against his, my nipples hardening against his cold skin.

"I'm going to taste you." He breathed the words nearly through me.

I didn't have time to understand what he meant before he dropped to his knees and threw one of my legs over his shoulder. I sucked in a breath now, knowing fully what kind of taste he was referring to. *Holy fucking shit.* Just as I was going to protest, mainly because I didn't think I could stand without my knees, he placed a strong hand on my belly to steady me. I couldn't help how damp I was growing. My core was throbbing with anticipation. A fact I was sure Cannon knew, because he seemed to be taking his damn time. Before I could grab the back of his head and push him forward, I felt a slow, confident lick along my wet folds. I think my goddamned eyes might have crossed, because the world went blurry at his first contact.

He made a noise much like a growl, but there was such a note of possession that it sent a shiver through my whole body. I tried desperately to grapple for what little sense I had left, but it was fleeting. Oddly, I was okay with that. My body wanted this and I was done denying it.

Cannon's tongue traced lazy circles around my swollen clit and I tried like hell to wiggle to get him to hit the damn target. But, true to Cannon, he would control even this. Without warning, he sucked the little bud into his mouth and my vision went completely black and someone screamed. He didn't let up. His tongue went from circles to probing just at my core and I couldn't seem to catch a breath.

He slipped his other hand between my legs and found my folds, spreading me wider to have better access to what he wanted. I couldn't help but arch up to him. I didn't need anything, but oh sweet torture, I wanted it all. He sucked me into his mouth once more and this time he didn't let up. I couldn't help but undulate under his assault. Then his finger moved to my entrance and, without hesitation, he thrust it inside of me.

My world fractured like a rock hitting a wind-shield, and then, with a few flicks of that wicked tongue, it flew apart completely. The orgasm hit me so hard I lost control. I heard that same person scream-ing and didn't have the strength to even keep myself standing.

Cannon kept a firm hand on me, as I'm sure he could understand that standing was not on the agen-da. He kissed his way up my torso, paused at my chest and gazed up at me. His eyes were all black and his fangs peeked out from his mischievous grin.

"I love the way you taste coming on my tongue," he huskily growled. I would have blushed had I been able, but it seemed as though I had little control. Words were too complex at that moment

"Your little body wants me. Let's give it what it wants, shall we?" He gave me a wicked grin as he stood up fully. I nodded. Or at least I thought I did.

I blinked rapidly to come back down from whatev-er it was I was floating on.

He pulled me down to the floor with my back flush against his chest. Both of us were on our knees and the carpet was digging into my skin, but I had little care.

My nipples were so painfully hard, that any other discomfort wasn't noticeable.

"Cannon, wait," I panted.

He froze. I glanced down at my chest to see his hand a breath away from my aching breast. I arched myself toward his seeking hand. Whatever protest or comment I had fell away with the electric contact of his hand. He sucked in a breath by my ear. Rolling my stiff peak between his finger and thumb, he thrust his hips forward, pressing his hard-as hell-erection against my lower back. I noticed that at some point he'd ditched his pants, so we were both naked. The feel of our skin together felt like ice meeting fire, like thousands of small static electric shocks all going off at every point of contact.

He flicked my right nipple, causing me to moan and push myself against him. Without missing a beat, he cupped my other heavy breast.

"Cannon, please," I begged. My core began to throb and grow with a need so strong I thought it would be impossible to elevate.

"What." He rolled my nipples with the word. "Do." He clamped down more firmly. "You." He licked my throat. "Want?" He ground his hardness against me.

"Say it, Addison. Say what you want."

I couldn't think with all of the stimulation. I tried to wiggle my ass against him, but that only made him snarl with what I assumed to be his own need. I knew he wanted me to say it so there could be no mistaking this. He was breaking down that last wall I held up.

"I want you inside of me," I whispered. It was all breath, because it was all need. What had started as want had turned into need — a need so strong that I couldn't even begin to want to stop it.

He slipped a hand from my breast down to my belly and down yet farther. The ache was building. The ache that I needed him to soothe, yet he moved so slowly. Teasing my skin, leaving an icy trail of fire in his wake. I distantly heard someone panting. I hated this position. I wanted to see him, touch him, learn him, yet with him at my back I could do nothing but accept what he wanted to give me. Nothing more, nothing less.

I felt his finger dip lower to slip between my drenched folds. My heart, which had been just shy of a jack hammer about to burst forth, nearly stopped at the contact. I sucked in a breath, trying to get some kind of oxygen into my system. I snaked a hand behind me to feel him. I reached low and was not disappointed. My fingers brushed the soft head of his erection.

I tried to stroke him, but with a groan, he snatched up my hand. In a blink, he had my other wrist pinned above my head against the wall just in front of me.

"Wha-" I didn't get the words out before he'd knocked my knees apart slightly. The sudden movement caused my back to hunch. I threw my left hand up to keep from hitting the wall. The action caused my body to lurch forward and my back to bow in an arch toward him.

Shifting his shaft so that it nestled so deliciously against my cleft, he began a slow rhythm of back and forth, running the velvety head against my clit every time. And every time, it chipped away what was left of my sanity. I shifted and he moved forward, causing him to breach my entrance for one perfect moment. I couldn't stifle the moan.

"Not yet," he panted huskily.

Please, god, please. I wanted to beg but somehow I resisted.

He continued his sensual back and forth. Soon, he moved one hand down to cup one of my breasts. I couldn't help but push the heavy mound fully into his hand. He found my nipple and pinched it, hard. I yelled. I simply couldn't help it.

Pausing his rhythm, I heard his voice in my mind, "*Addison, I need to feel your heat around me.*"

He didn't give me time to respond before I felt what I'd felt just moments ago: his broad head pushing firmly at my entrance. I said a silent prayer that he wouldn't stop this time. He didn't. He pushed himself inside of me so slowly, he left behind a burning sensation as my body tried to accommodate his large size.

"So fucking tight," he moaned.

He paused, knowing my body needed a moment to get used to him. I exhaled a breath.

He was holding so much of his dominant personality back in that moment, though I needed everything he had to offer. I wiggled back, easing myself down on him farther.

"I'm trying to be gentle with you, but if you keep doing that, I'm going to-"

I did it again. His grip on my hands tightened and he thrust himself the rest of the way in. My vision blurred from the pain, ecstasy and feeling of satisfaction.

He paused. I could practically hear him berating himself.

"I need just who you are, Cannon. Not who you think I need you to be."

He needed to control this, I knew it. And I loved it. There was this part of me that wanted to give this up to him. I always had. I had no idea what would happen beyond this, but I wasn't sure it mattered or that I cared. Moving my hands from the wall to behind his neck and shifting my body upward, he growled in my ear, "Don't let go."

He was now supporting my weight, a position that was about his control. He withdrew himself, and just when I thought he would slip out completely he impaled me. He continued like that, slow, almost methodical withdrawal, and then a heated, hard penetration. Over and over. I could feel myself building to a peak and wanted nothing more than for him to shove me so far off that edge that I'd never see it again, parachute be damned. His hands went from working my nipples to squeezing my small breasts. Every time he would pull out, he rubbed my bared mounds, and every time he shoved into me, he twisted my nipples, nearing pain but never quite making it there.

He was keeping me on the edge. I began meeting him thrust for thrust, picking up the pace because my body had all but taken over in its search for release.

Moving his left hand to my chin, he tilted my head, giving him access to my neck. I knew what he wanted. And God knew I wanted it too.

I moaned the only word I could ever seem to say with him. "Yes."

His fangs sank so deep inside of me it felt like a thrust of his cock. Each time he pulled on the small wound, it sent wave after wave to my sex, causing me to clench around him. I was so damn close. His thrusts became more frantic. My control had long gone and it seemed his was slipping as well.

His hand moved from my breast to my lower belly, then found its way to my swollen clit. It was all too much. His thrusts, his bite, and now the fingers between my legs. I couldn't hold on any longer. That precipice that I'd been dangling off of, I was just shoved over. I came in a wet rush.

I didn't even care to stop the screams that were ripped out of my throat. I felt him pulse deep inside of me. He bit down harder on my flesh, as if he knew I needed it; the deep fracture that had splintered the fragile glass of my world flew apart into millions of tiny shards.

I don't think I'd ever had a climax so intense in my whole life. My hearing had gone completely and all of the muscles in my body had turned to jelly.

At some point, when I was coming back into my body, I'd been eased down to the bed. I peered up to the ceiling, hoping to clear my vision back into focus.

"Addison," a voice broke through the fog. I turned

my head in search of the sound. Cannon lay on his side; the look on his face puzzled me. His eyes were focused and his lips were pinched into a while line. He looked worried. I frowned.

"What's wrong?" I asked.

"You're crying," he said in much the same tone one would use with a frightened deer. I reached up to my cheek, felt slight dampness, and pulled my fingers away to inspect them. I saw the slick glistening of wetness. *Lord help me.* Heat rushed to my cheeks. I had no words.

"Sometimes, Addison, you don't need words," he informed me just before crushing his lips against mine.

I wasn't sure what the hell had just happened, but I did know this might have been the biggest mistake I'd ever made.

Chapter Nineteen

bsolute disappointment was plastered all over his face. His beautiful features were drawn and he was peering at me as though he didn't know who I was. I could see his rage spill over through the ice of his eyes. They flicked from light blue to nearly white with his strong emotion. His jaw flexed as he gnashed his teeth. I could not, for the life of me, understand why he was so upset with me. I mean, I didn't think I'd pissed in his Cheerios, but it was possible.

"GODDAMN YOU, ADDISON!" he kept screaming over and over again, his Scottish accent more pronounced than I'd ever heard it. I tried like hell to ask him why he was so mad, but he kept yelling the same three words over and over.

After about ten minutes of his insistent yelling, I realized his gaze shifted from me to a space just over my shoulder and back again. I turned my head and blinked at the man standing there.

I woke up in a sudden gasp for air, one I needed

and had to have right then. I sat up half expecting to be yelled at. The dark room was spinning in a swirling mass of grays and blacks. I felt cool hands clench my shoulders and jerked in response. I did not, in any way, want to be touched. *What is wrong with me?*

I lurched from the bed as if my ass was on fire. I had no idea what exactly I was running from. My eyes were burning from interrupted sleep and my head was spinning from the confusion. It didn't help that my sleep schedule had been so messed up.

As soon as my body left the bed and my feet hit the carpet, I fell to the floor with a dull thud, gasping for air and grasping for clarity. I willed my heart to slow. Rubbing my eyes, my vision cleared somewhat.

"Morning-after regrets?" Cannon's words filled my addled brain one syllable at a time. Much like a life raft, I rode them in until I was able to fully understand what the hell had happened.

"No," I rasped. Though, I wasn't one hundred percent sure about that. I couldn't meet his eyes. *God, what is wrong with me?*

Getting up from the floor, I made my way to the bathroom, pausing at the doorway and asking over my shoulder, "Hey, can Lachlan enter into humans dreams like you can?" I didn't know what I wanted his answer to be.

"No, not that I know of."

I turned and headed straight for the shower. I needed to sift through all of these feelings and emotions without having Cannon breathing down my neck.

I glanced at my clothes, which at some point had been scooped up and folded neatly, on the counter. I hadn't read the letter that Evie sent me, so I went digging for it. My fingers brushed the pink paper, but for some reason, I paused not pulling it out.

"Cannon, we have a problem." My tone was grave.

"What?" he called from the other room. I heard rustling and the creak of the bed. I turned to face him. He was still nude and very, very happy to see me. I turned away. Not that I was shy, just … I don't really know why. I guess it just seemed like the right thing to do. Thank dear sweet little baby Jesus he didn't say anything about it.

"Well?" he asked while clearing his throat. *Oh shit right.*

"Oh, yeah. Okay, going to that address could be an issue."

"Why?"

"We don't know what's there. What if the Litch is there? How would we go about killing him? It's not like we have the Litch's stone. How should we go about killing something that can't be killed?" This had been bothering me for some time. Just where would one hide one's soul? If it were me, I would drop it down a hole in Siberia. This was a huge detail. One I had no idea how to even go about addressing.

"I have no idea," he grumbled as he walked away.

Well, wasn't that a productive conversation?

I walked back to Evie's letter and slipped it out of the envelope. Glitter spilled out of the pale-pink folded paper from either side. I rolled my eyes at the sparkled mess covering my bare toes and opened the paper, causing yet more pink glitter to fall.

Her handwriting was a mess and I had to start and stop the whole way through to decipher. It didn't help that she wrote in a purple pen with even more damn glitter in it.

"Addison,

Don't you just love glitter? It's just so fucking sparkly! I forgot to tell you a few things when you left. I know, silly me! First, good going getting that D! Rwar!"

I paused at that particular tidbit. *What the? You know, I don't even want to know.*

"Before you go to that place, you know the one in the other letter. You need something. What was it called?"

A Litch stone? I added mentally.

"*Oh yes sorry, a Litch stone.*"

I sighed at the letter. *How the fuck is she doing that?*

"*I might be able to help with that. You need to go have a look in the tree house. Oh wait. Maybe under the tree. Anyway, you know the one I mean. Theo you'll need to take. Oh goodness I'm totally channeling Yoda!*"

Really? I shook my head, unable to stop my lips from twitching up into a small smile. Helpful Evie was; however, clear and to the point, not so much.

"*Not that it will really help. The stone is just a little thing in your way. Two will still die and you will pull the trigger. A stone can't help you do that. It's all on you.*"

My heart sank. I didn't know what all of this meant! It was beyond frustrating!

"*You're going to fall hard, Addison. Make sure you are prepared to lose everything. Not that you could help it at this point. It's already started. Oh and happy early birthday!*"

I rolled my eyes. My birthday was coming up. Not really something I was all too happy with. The day of lovers. Valentine's Day. What a shitty birthday. I glanced back at the letter to finish it.

"*Okay bye! Evie.*"

Trying to read that letter was like arguing with a three-year-old. An act in futility, or so I've seen with my limited experience. I set the pink parchment down on the sink and peered down at my feet.

I looked as though I'd been following a particularly gassy unicorn. I sparkled like a freaking disco ball. It wasn't exactly a look I wanted.

Walking toward the shower, I paused to view the time on the small, yet ornately designed clock. There was filigree of gold and silver that twisted on the sides and there were deep-red stones that seemed to drip off like small droplets of blood. It was a stunning little thing.

The clock face read 6:26 a.m. I had a little more than twelve hours before I needed to be at the house of horrors. A shiver erupted over my whole body. I had to lean against the cold marble wall to help steady myself. Flashbacks of my childhood seemed to always hit me so hard that I thought I'd be taken down to my knees. I never wanted to relive the feelings of nothingness and self-loathing, but I wasn't sure I'd ever move on completely from them. As much as I always say that I shouldn't let my past cripple me, that's exactly what has happened. I was completely crippled, damaged beyond repair. I may look normal but I felt anything but.

I shook my head and pushed off the wall. I needed

the shower more than anything right now. I need the hot water to melt off the past few days of pure shit. Reaching out, I turned the lever all the way to the left. The rain head turned on full blast and I had to jump out of the way to avoid being blasted by freezing water.

After a few moments, the large stall filled up with steam and I stepped in. The heat of the water burned my exposed skin, but I didn't really care.

My original intention with this shower was to stay in until the water ran cold. Apparently Cannon's water heater was the size of an army tank. So, I settled in for a while, or when my fair skin turned about as red as a well-done lobster. The lobster won.

The shower, unfortunately, didn't wash away all of the shit that seemed to pile up around me. I sighed.

I looked at the mirror which, surprisingly, wasn't covered in condensation. My blue eyes shined like bright aquamarines. *I guess red really suits me.* Pulling the soft white towel around me, I made my way over to my clothes.

I had to tell Cannon I needed to go to my old tree house. Well, it wasn't really a tree house. It was four or five wooden planks set between two trees. But, it was mine. It was where I went when I was taken from my mother and brother. Aaron knew about it and always told me to meet him there if I got lost. I went there every day for years and he never came for me. He never once showed up. Like all the rest, he'd abandoned me.

I punched the reflection before me, praying I would shatter everything about who I was. The glass splintered into a large spider web. My refection was now exactly what I expected it should be. Distorted. There were small drops of blood running down the fractured mirror. I glanced at my hand. I hadn't felt the pain or, rather, I didn't care about it.

"Cannon, I'm sorry you don't like it, but one," I held up a finger, "you need to sleep. You'll be of no use to anyone, including the forty vampires you're organizing to storm the castle, if you're not at your best." I held up another finger. "And two, Evie told me to take Theo. And, as much as she's a few songs short of a disco, I've kinda come to think maybe I should listen to her."

His jaw clenched and I saw that I'd won the argument. He scoffed something unintelligible and threw up his hands. I knew that him not going wasn't the main issue. But I wasn't ready to talk about what had happened between us. He'd brought it up a few times, and I'd sidestepped that conversation like a game of dodgeball. The truth was, I wasn't sure how I felt about Cannon. I mean, I liked him and felt a connection, but I still had lingering feelings for Lachlan. *I've royally fucked up this whole situation, typical Addison style.* I needed to see how we all came out on the other side before I could make any decisions. Besides, it wasn't like Cannon was looking for a wife. Fuck that. I wasn't looking to be a wife. I shuddered at the thought.

"Theo is still recovering," Cannon muttered.

"I know that, but Evie-"

"I'll be fine," Theo's smooth, calm-as-ever voice echoed through the hallway.

Cannon and I turned to face the tall man walking toward us in the bar room.

"How?" I asked. Meaning how the hell had he known to come here?

"Evie sent me a letter. Took me about two hours to get the glitter out of my carpet." He laughed his low, rumbling sound.

I wanted to run to him, wanted to throw myself in his arms and tell him how shitty of a person I was and how sorry I was.

"Hey, chickadee." He smirked down at me.

"Hey."

"Well, now that the pleasantries are over, how

about we go through a plan of the next few hours. And maybe only fifty percent of us will die," Cannon spat. I rolled my eyes at his tone.

"You know, you could be nice," I scolded, though my heart wasn't in it. Evie's words flash in my mind. *Two will still die and you will pull the trigger.* I tried to swallow back the fear, but it was still there. I didn't want anyone to die. Okay, aside from the prick who took my friends. I could only hope that I would be one of the ones to die. I didn't want anyone caught up in a mess that, despite everything, seemed to be about me.

I paused. Why did this money man want the Litch dead? I mean, clearly he did, or why else would he be "helping" me? Maybe he helped create him and has lost control? Or maybe he didn't? That didn't feel right. I was willing to bet that the money man created the pusher-vampire hybrids and the Litch. Then he lost control of them. Now, he's doing cleanup on all of the collateral damage.

But, why me? It had to be Jack. He had to have sent this twat donkey the results of my blood work and that's what started all of this. I love when my stupidity comes back to bite me in the ass, assuming all of this was true and not just the rambling thoughts of an over-exhausted crazy person.

"Addison."

I looked up and saw both Cannon and Theo blinking at me as though they'd asked a question. *Oops.*

"Sorry, what?"

"Addison, if you're not going to pay attention then we will leave you here," Cannon chided.

His petulant tone pissed me off. I was not a child. But, if I huffed at him, I would absolutely be seen as one.

"Cannon, she's not a child." Theo's tone was low and controlled. I looked over at him. I wasn't used to having someone stick up for me. I had to fight to keep the grin off my face.

"Look, we don't have a whole lot of time to sit here and be petty assholes. So, Theo and I will go over to the tree house while you and the 'fuck em up squad' go check out the … house." I had a hard time choking out the word. It had always been a dungeon. A place that I spent so many nights praying to a God I no longer believed in. Praying, fuck, begging for him to save me. He never did. I survived so that I could save myself. That thought alone seemed to inject some much-needed iron into my bones.

Cannon's eyes pinched shut. He didn't seem convinced at all. Not that I really blamed him. Pretty much everything I came up with turned into a cluster-fuck one way or another. But, it wasn't like our cups over-runneth with options.

Flexing his jaw, Cannon muttered, "I don't like splitting up."

"Well, I don't like jelly donuts. But, when that's all that's left and I'm hungry, it's what I eat."

"Did you really just equate this situation to a jelly donut?" Theo asked incredulously.

"Okay that may not have been my best moment. How about, 'Suck it up, buttercup.' That better?"

"Not really."

I shrugged.

"Cannon." He looked at me fully. "We're running out of time and options. While Lachlan can hold on and survive whatever this Litch is dishing out, Darryl is human. He can't. We have to go and finish this, now." My tone was harsh, but my emotions were grave.

"She's right," Theo added.

"I know she's right!" Cannon snapped. His eyes never left mine. He seemed to want to say more, though he didn't.

He walked over to me and placed a hand on my cheek. There was some emotion I couldn't name that flashed across his face. I was struck so hard with the need to run, but I choked it back.

"Be careful," he whispered. This was too close. He was getting too close. He leaned down for what I assumed would be a kiss. I ducked under his chin and twisted out of his light touch. I couldn't handle it, not in that moment.

Theo's eyes locked on mine and he turned toward the door. I had the distinct feeling that the panic I felt was projected on my face. I felt Cannon's iron grip circle around my upper arm. I tried to pull away, causing him to squeeze tighter.

"Addison." He paused. I looked at him, meeting his dark eyes. "I'm not asking for you to talk about what happened last night. I'm not even asking for it to happen ever again. But, I won't be a regret. I won't be a weakness. Addison, you need to figure out this shit. You need to decide what it is that you want."

I swallowed the now California-sized lump in my throat. He was right, of course he was right. I had no idea what I wanted. Everything was so muddled. But, regret? No, I don't think I was there yet.

"Cannon, I don't regret what happened. I'm just confused. There's a lot going on and right now there isn't time for me, you, or anything. We barely have time to go get my friends and pray to some benevolent god whom I don't believe in that we don't die in the process." My tone shifted from even to harsh.

Releasing my arm, Cannon walked over to the window. No words were spoken. There was nothing more either of us could have said or wanted to say. So, with that I turned, made my way to the front door, and when I walked out I didn't look back.

Chapter Twenty

"Okay, chickadee, where am I driving us to?" Theo asked, heading south on 285. I gave him directions and his normally cheerful smile faded, slowly turning into a scowl.

I returned my attention to the cars passing by. They blurred into streaks of lights as they passed, going the opposite direction. Running that fast had replaced heroin for me. It was just as much of an addiction though. My mind blanks, my skin tingles, my heart pounds so hard in my chest it distorts my vision, my body releases endorphins so my limbs and muscles can accommodate what I need them to. I logically knew replacing one addiction with another could only, in time, cause a relapse, but I wasn't worried. At least that's what I told myself.

"That's a rough neck of the woods."

I tuned to face Theo.

"What is?" I asked, then understanding what he was referring to I quickly added, "Yeah, it's not far from the shithole I used to live in."

"You know, I'm no pusher. But I'm pretty good at reading people. And I know you."

I was trying to listen to him, but the closer we got to our destination, the louder my heart beat got, drowning out nearly everything.

"When are you gunna tell me about why we're goin here? About why this guy has a major hard-on for you?"

I sighed. It wasn't that I wanted to keep anything from him, I just didn't want to tell him everything. I didn't want to tell anyone. However, I knew if I didn't, Theo could get hurt, again. I absolutely did not want that to happen, ever.

Taking in a deep breath, I explained about the tree. I explained about the house where I was assuming the Litch was. And I explained why I never wanted to go there again. He never pushed me.

"Where did you go after that home?" he asked in a bare whisper.

"Well, I bounced around from a few different homes, but eventually I landed with my aunt and uncle. And if that home was hell, then theirs was something so far beyond it hasn't been named."

The skin on his dark jaw tightened, causing his

• 2 8 5 •

features to pull as he gritted his teeth. His eyes were focused on the turns and lights. His hands held a death grip on the wheel, his knuckles turning nearly white.

I returned my attention to the cars and dilapidated buildings. I would say they'd been nice when I was young, but they'd always looked like something out of a post-apocalyptic world. Yup, this is what I remember. No pink ponies and rainbow-shitting unicorns for me. Dirty discarded crack pipes and broken glass littered streets.

We sat in silence the rest of the ride. Me not really knowing what to say and him clearly fighting the urge to ask too much.

Pointing to an old, abandoned drug store, I choked, "There. Park there."

He pulled off the street, being careful not to run over the small group of kids who couldn't have been more than about nine. He parked and we both got out.

Eyeing the kids I suggested, "You may want to lock your car."

He glanced at the group and scoffed, but then thought better of it and locked it.

Good. I knew the lives these kids had and I thought between myself and them, I got lucky when I was taken from my mom. They were forced to grow up there.

I led Theo behind the drugstore, to a thicket of overgrown grass and weeds. There was a smattering of dead trees that littered the area but we were looking for two close together. Two that, last I recalled, had been alive. One of the two I couldn't put my arms around because it was so big. Or at least it had been when I was a kid.

I paused, struggling to remember what everything looked like. So much had changed. But, surprisingly, some things had stayed the same. Then, just off to my left, I saw a large tree, maybe not as big as I remember, but still pretty damn big. These two trees somehow were still alive and were the only ones that still held on to their hand-sized brown leaves. It honestly made my heart happy to see that one thing from the awful place made it out alive and virtually unchanged.

There were boards about fifty feet up from the ground that lay spread between that tree and the smaller one next to it. I smiled. It wasn't the castle that I imagined it to be when I was young, but it was still there. That's all that mattered.

"That's it," I said, pointing to it.

"What? Oh, um, that?" he asked, not understanding then pointing to the wooden planks.

Nodding, I added, "Well, to a five-year-old it was

a castle with a moat and fifteen vicious alligators." I shoved his shoulder and tried to laugh slightly, hoping to lighten the mood. He just chuckled uncomfortably.

"Theo, I had a terrible childhood. I don't want it to impact how you see me. How you feel about me." He stopped and turned to me, his face drawn and grave.

"Addison, it's not that. It's the fact that what you told me is awful. So awful that anyone would have had a hard time making sense of life and likely taken the path you did. But, I have a hard time knowing that what you told me was likely not the worst. Not by a long shot. I know there's more and it's likely so bad that I'll wonder how you're still breathing." His voice held an edge of sorrow mixed with desperation.

I didn't know what to say, so I said nothing. He was right. It wasn't near the worst. More importantly, he didn't need to know. It no longer mattered. I am who I am not because of what happened, but because of how I chose to move on from it.

"How would you suggest we get up there?" Theo asked, eyeing the narrow platform.

"Leave that to me. I guess you just look on the ground? Evie wasn't really clear."

"Why am I not surprised?" He laughed the question because it was so true.

I returned my attention to the tree. When I was a kid there had been small slats of wood nailed along the tree's trunk. These small steps seemed to have gone the way of the dodo. I looked up at the tree. Though it looked a hell of a lot smaller than I remembered, it would still be difficult to climb.

There were no low-lying limbs to even grasp onto, so climbing the normal way was out. I sighed, knowing I would have to levitate myself up. I'd only done this once and it didn't really end well.

I cleared my mind and focused on my feet. I knew how the ability worked. I knew that it was like a muscle, in that if I didn't use it I became unreliable and weak. Glancing up at the planks, I focused on the distance between the two. I pulled hard on the rope that was my ability. Nothing happened. I pulled harder, trying to shape and bend the world to what I wanted, to what I needed. Still, nothing happened. I let out a breath. I couldn't understand why this ability worked like magic sometimes and other times it was utter crap.

I was doing something wrong. I mean, every pusher's ability was totally unique to them and the same went for how they used it. Someone else who had telekinetic abilities would use their power way differently than I would. So, there was no right or wrong way.

I glanced up to the beams again. This time, I pulled on them. Reaching out with my hands, I bent the world once again, attempting to close the distance. The pressure on my feet lessened as the gap between my outstretched fingers and the wooden planks closed. I was a hair away before I felt my power slipping. *Oh no you don't*! I pulled hard on that invisible rope. I pulled a little too hard, as it turns out. I went flying into the air, way past my target. A good twenty feet past, in fact.

"Oh shit!" slipped out of my mouth as I began falling toward the Earth. I reached for the boards and was able to grab one with both forearms. I scrambled to pull myself up. Once I was fully on the beams I sat for a moment, attempting to reinflate my lungs. I held my hands up to my face. They were shaking. *For fuck's sake, Addison, you need to use that ability more before you kill yourself!*

After a moment, I got to my feet and paced the small expanse. There was nothing I could see up here. *But, if his Litch stone was here, the questions I have are why? And how would he know about this place?*

Why in the world have the very thing that could kill you so close to you? Why not just sink it at the bottom of the ocean? And, damn, why here? That was the main question for me.

I spent hours up here just after I was taken from my mother. I would run away from whatever house I was placed in and wait here, unmoving with my little feet dangling off. I waited for Aaron, my brother, who'd always been a hero, to come save me. I remembered yelling his name, willing him to appear. He never did. Just another in the long line of people who let me down. After a few years, I stopped coming. I stopped believing in everything, especially a savior.

I continued to pace the space. Back and forth. There was nothing up here, but I couldn't seem to pull my head out of the past long enough to get down. So, instead, I looked up.

Above me were dead limbs with not a leaf to be seen. I stared and narrowed my eyes. Hanging on about twenty of the branches were small to medium-sized bags. They were purple from what I could see and made of some kind of cloth. My mouth gaped open. How the flying hell was I supposed to get all of these and how would I know which one contained this tampon biter's soul?

I would have to use my ability to pull each of these baggies down. Wonderful, just wonderful. Small bags full of rocks potentially flying at my face. What could possibly go wrong? I groaned at the thought.

"Addison!" Theo called.

I looked down and saw Theo's bright smile peering up at me. I couldn't help but grin stupidly back at him. He'd always, well as long as I'd known him, been one of those people whose happiness was infectious.

"What up?" I asked.

"I have good news and bad news." His tone held an amused note.

"Wonderful. What's the good news?"

"I found something."

I already knew what the bad news was but I let him finish.

"But, the bad news is I think I've found about thirty somethings. All wrapped up in pretty little velvet bags."

"Ughhhh," I groaned in response. No wonder this guy didn't care if we found his hiding spot. He had fifty decoys planted along with the real thing. So, even if we did "find" it, we had to figure out a way to tell if we had the right one. I thought about just smashing every one of them and just killing him that way. No fight needed. But, I figured he had a safeguard in place to kill Darryl and Lachlan. This guy, whoever he was, was insane but not dumb.

This is going to be impossible.

I returned my attention to the little baggies that hung so delicately on the dead branches of the trees. It struck me as a macabre Christmas tree, with the purple and wine-colored ornaments seeming to drip like large drops of blood.

"Hey, watch out below," I called.

I raised my arms above my head and mentally grabbed a hold of about half of the little bags. I pulled my arms downward as I mentally did the same. The stones flew down, some bouncing on the plank and some rocketing like bullets to the ground. I did the same for the rest of the dangling velvet bags. I then gathered the little pouches and tossed them one by one to Theo.

"ADDISON!" Cannon's pained voice screamed in my mind. I fell to my knees with the searing pain of the connection we shared.

"Chickadee?! What's wrong?" Theo's panicked voice filtered in around the pain in my mind. My eyes flooded with tears that I couldn't control.

It was at that moment I felt the fiery pain of our connection severing. I screamed, but held on to consciousness. Fighting against the agony, I clawed my way out of the darkness that threatened to overwhelm me.

"Cannon." I was able to gasp his name just before another wave of fire lit me from the inside out. I was curled into the fetal position, trying like hell to find a way to make this pain subside. It didn't. But I refused to pass out. I needed to hold on.

"Our connection-" Another wave stronger than before washed over me. I couldn't help but scream.

"Addison, I need you to roll off of that plank. I'll catch you, but-"

I didn't let him finish his panicked words. I simply rolled off and didn't care if he caught me or not. The free fall, the weightlessness, eased the burning pain slightly. For that brief moment, I was granted a small reprieve. It didn't last long.

I slammed into Theo's outstretched arms. The force of the impact caused me to bite down on my tongue and my mouth to fill with blood. The torment from before hit me tenfold.

I was losing the battle to stay awake.

"Addison, you need to let go of this pain," Theo's smooth voice cajoled me into a calmer state. His words sank in fully. I didn't think anyone, no matter how strong they were, could mentally, physically, or emotionally withstand this pain. I let go and sank into the darkness. Distantly, I thought I heard a man's voice laughing. But as I sank fast and hard to escape the agony, I couldn't be sure of anything other than deliverance from that pain.

"*Addison, I need you.*"

I sat straight up, gasping for air. The voice that woke me had been the one I needed. It'd been Lachlan. My vision was fuzzy and my body felt as though I'd been hit by a truck, then, just for good measure, the bastard had backed over me a few times and set me on fire.

"Hey you're up," Theo's voice broke through the throbbing in my head.

"Yeah," was all I could manage. I blinked to clear my vision enough to see where I was. Slowly, the world shifted into focus. I was in the backseat of his car.

I opened my mouth to ask how long I'd been out, but the words caught in my dry throat.

Theo, who I realized wasn't driving, held up a hand.

"You've been out for a few hours, but not long."

Shit. We didn't have much time. I had to be at that house in a few hours. Light spilled into the car from both the full moon and the amber glow of the only working streetlight.

I tried to not think about what the severed connection to Cannon meant. I tried not to think about the fact that it likely meant he was dead. Trying to swallow the lump in my throat, I sat up. I squeezed my eyes shut as I did so. As if that would help ease the pain. It didn't.

"Whoa, Addison. Lay down."

I shook my head at him. That brought on a wave of nausea. I pushed down the compulsion to wretch.

"We have to get to the house and figure out which of the goddamned things is the Litch stone." My voice was stronger than it had been, but it still sounded pained even to my ears.

"Addison-"

"No. I don't care. I don't have a choice. Time isn't running out, it's run out." I didn't even try to call him, though I desperately wanted to know if he was okay. I knew calling could do more harm than good.

Nodding he explained, "I know, but there are fifty-seven stones. All different colors, sizes, and kinds." He turned fully in his seat before saying, "We have no way of knowing which stone is his. Unless you want to just smash all of them."

Shaking my head, I said, "No. I'm sure he has plans set in place if he were to just drop dead. That won't work. We need to figure this out."

I couldn't just run into this guns blazing, like I

tended to do. There were too many lives at stake. An image of Cannon with a smirk warming his normally cool face flashed in my mind. *If they weren't already dead.*

"Let's lay it all out," Theo murmured, opening the driver's side door.

"What, ugh-" I pulled myself up and opened my door. "What do you mean?"

I swung my feet out and had to take a breather. *I really hope all this Litch wants to do was have some hot tea and a bubble bath, because I'm pretty useless right now.*

I somehow managed to pull my heavy body out of the car and to my feet. *Had gravity increased while I was out?*

I turned my face up toward the full moon. All of the burnt oranges, pinks, and purples of the fading day had swirled and started to fade to the darkest of blues. We were running out of time. Returning my attention to Theo, I made my way over to the front of the car. I ran a hand along the cold surface of the vehicle, trying to wake up my sleeping nerve endings. The warmer day had chilled into a fairly brisk night, yet I still felt hot and overheated.

Theo was emptying each baggie and setting its contents on the car's hood. There were six rows of rocks. Some looked to be the same shape, color, and basic size, whereas others were vastly different. Just looking at them, I felt defeated. I had no idea what I was looking for or how I could possibly figure this out.

"Well?" Theo asked. Clearly he thought I had all the answers.

"Boy, we are screwed," I scoffed.

"Yeah, I kinda got that feeling."

I walked over to the first stone and ran my fingers along it. It was about the size of a quarter. It was smooth and a deep chocolate color. It reminded me a bit of a river rock. The damn thing would make one hell of a skipping stone. I picked it up and inspected it in the moonlight. It had the smallest veins of gold running through the center splintering off to the edges.

There were about four other stones that were similar.

Putting the stone back, I confessed in an exasperated tone, "You know I have no idea what I'm looking for, right?"

"Yeah, I figured that. If it helps I have no idea either." He sighed.

It didn't. The size of the stones varied from about the size of my fist to as small as a dime. Some were white and others were a deep onyx and the rest were every color and shade between.

"I think we will just have to look at all of them." I sighed as well, not really liking that idea.

Theo nodded and picked up a stone. I did the same.

Fourteen stones later I was about ready to just run them all over with the car and hope it just all worked out.

"We're spending too much time on this. And it's not like we know what we're looking for. I'm not getting a spidey tingle about any of these damn things." I plopped the fist-sized purple stone on the car's hood with a thunk.

Theo held up another fist-sized white stone. He turned the quartz-looking rock over and it seemed to catch the light and reflect it as he moved it. He held it still for a moment, the moonlight hitting it just right, and I gaped at it. It looked as if there was a small glowing swirl spinning in the center of the rock. I very nearly launched myself over the car and snatched the stone out of his hand.

"You could have-" His words stopped altogether when I held up the stone. His eyes widened and a small smile spread across his face.

"Get all of the others like this one," I instructed, unable to take my eyes off the white, glowing swirls of light.

"There are two others similar to this one." He held up one in each hand. I crossed the car and closed the distance between us. Holding the two stones up against the moonlight, we both studied them intently. One of the stones had a thin line of black running through the center of it. The other looked nearly identical to the glowing one but it had a pale purplish tint to it.

"These are pretty, but they aren't glowing," Theo remarked.

Nodding, I began to formulate a plan. Well, maybe plan was too strong of a word. I should have called it a "just in case my ass was toast" kinda thing. I shoved the glowing rock into my right pocket and grabbed the other two and shoved them in my left. I looked like a shoplifter, but I really didn't care.

"Those rocks in your pants or are you just happy to see me?" he joked, but I couldn't find the humor in it at that moment. All I could see was the memory of Theo's lifeless body crumpling to the ground. My heart began to pound so hard I thought it might come marching out through my chest. I would never see Theo or anyone I love in that condition because of me ever again.

Theo met my eyes. His gaze was pulled tight and I looked away.

"Oh no you don't." He shook his head as he spoke the words.

"Theo…" I chided.

"No freaking way, chickadee. You're not leaving me out of this."

Damn him. He didn't give me a chance to respond before he closed his door and locked it. I brushed the rocks off the hood of the car and made my way over to my door. It was still locked.

Leaning down, I narrowed my eyes at him. He shook his head in firm negation. I sighed.

"Theo, the last time you almost died-"

"Do I wear big boy underwear?" he asked. He had to yell the question through the closed window.

I just blinked at him, having been caught off-guard by the question.

"Uhhhh, I mean, I don't honestly know. I've never seen you in, um, that state before?" I hesitantly responded.

"Look, I'm a big boy and thus I wear big boy underwear. I can make my own choices."

"Or mistakes," I added. He scowled at me but I ignored him. I tried the door again. "Theo, please."

Shaking his head, he yelled, "No. Not until you agree that I wear big boy underwear."

I rolled my eyes and had to bite my lower lip to keep from smiling.

I looked around to make sure no one was around when I yelled back, "Theo, you wear big boy panties!"

I couldn't stop myself from laughing. Distantly, I heard the telltale click of the door unlocking.

"You just had to go there, didn't you?" he chortled.

"My way or the highway, right?"

Scoffing he said, "Something like that," just as he pulled off onto the road.

Chapter Twenty-One

"What the hell kind of plan is that?" Theo asked, eyeing me. I, however, couldn't tear my attention away from the dilapidated house. It'd been nicer when I was a child. Well, by nicer I mean not falling down one shingle or beam at a time.

This was the first home I'd been sent to after I was taken away from my mother. I thought that this would be a place where I would just wait for my mom to come for me. She never did. Then came the news she was dead. Even as a child, I wasn't surprised. She'd chosen her addiction over me, and what was left of my tiny heart broke every day Aaron didn't rescue me. I could have withstood the beatings and being locked in the closet for days, but what truly broke my child's mind was knowing my only hero discarded me like trash.

I had to blink away tears of old hurt. I refused to let this affect me, refused to fall down that abyss of bullshit. I wasn't a child. I was beyond that former pain.

"It's a shit plan. That's why I told you to not come. You're a lowly human." I turned to study his face. His concern shifted hesitantly to amusement and his hand flew to his forehead.

"You wound me so deep, chickadee," he huffed in mock hurt.

I rolled my eyes. I wanted so badly to duct tape him to the car so he couldn't get out, but he was a big boy, as he'd mentioned.

"All right you, got them big boy panties pulled up?"

"Up high and tight. Let's hope I don't shit them."

"One can hope."

Walking up to the door, I felt a number of mixed emotions. I felt strong and determined. Yet, I felt cautious. I could feel people in the house. I just knew they were there. Though I couldn't tell quite how many, I still knew this wouldn't be a walk in the park.

The once-red door was splintered and weathered, leaving only the barest hint of the formerly welcoming color. The yard was so overgrown that we very nearly needed a machete to hack through it. That overgrowth looked to be only a few days away from consuming the whole porch.

Pausing just in front of the warped door, I asked, "Do we knock?"

Theo's only response was a loud snort. I agreed. We were beyond politeness.

I squeezed the latch on the handle and pushed the door open. I'm not sure what I was expecting, but I certainly wasn't thinking the damn door would fall off the hinges and go careening to the floor.

The fall happened in slow motion, while the sound erupted as if it were a shot from a gun. I jumped at the audible intrusion. I couldn't help it. It nearly scared the piss out of me. It's not like my nerves were made of iron at that point.

"Well, that was fun," Theo whispered.

When stepping into the house, I had to walk over the poor door. I could almost feel for the wooden plank. Everyone beating on you, and here you are expected to withstand and pull through. But, at some point you just can't, and your hinges give out. I wondered how close my hinges were to giving out. *How long would it take for me to be the one on the ground?*

The house itself was much like the outside: rundown. Besides splintered wood and peeling wallpaper, I didn't see anyone or even any evidence that anyone'd been here in a very long time. I continued through the narrow hallway, past the closet where I'd been locked in for hours to days, for my unfortunate "bad attitude."

The kitchen had always been a large expanse that as a child I'd been forced to maintain in a meticulous manor. Now, however, it was in ruin. It looked as though a fire had ripped through it, leaving behind a charred shell of its former self.

I felt a tap on my shoulder and whirled to face it, my heart nearly exploding through my chest. It was Theo pointing at a door that was ajar just behind me. On the doorframe, above my head, hung a paper. Theo reached up and pulled it down. His eyes went wide then he handed it to me. It was my name, ADDY, written in crayon with purple flowers, snowflakes, and red hearts. The once-white paper had yellowed over time and it had started to flake around the edges. There were creases along the middle indicating it'd been folded up for some time. The paper I'd drawn when I first arrived here. It had hung on my door.

My mouth gaped open as I stared at it. I couldn't understand how it was here after all this time. How had it not been crumpled up and discarded? And why the hell was it here?

"I made this when I was little. When I first got here. It hung on my door," I told Theo.

"Well, I guess someone wants you to go down to the base-" His words were interrupted by a blood-curdling scream echoing up from the darkened stairwell. We shared a brief glance before I bolted down. I slammed shoulder first into the wall just beyond the end of the last step, not turning fast enough.

Clearing my vision, I scrambled to my feet and came face to face with the monster. One of my plans had been to charge and not let him give me some long diatribe. But my feet wouldn't move. I couldn't even blink.

My mouth went dry. My mind rebelled against what my eyes were seeing. I almost retched at the sight of him. His skin was so pale I would have thought someone would have taken him to the morgue. The skin on his fine-featured face hung loosely in some places and in others it had started to peel off, leaving huge patches of black necrotic flesh. His hair was blond in the patches that weren't missing. And he was tall. So much taller than I recalled.

But, his eyes. I could have gotten past the grotesque state of his appearance, but his blue eyes that once had a spark of defiance and childlike mischief were dead and dull. They mirrored my own at the lowest point in my life. His lips twisted into a mangled smirk. Half of his bottom lip was missing, leaving a gaping hole of gray flesh and blackened teeth. His stench nearly knocked me over.

When I was a kid, I saw a cat get hit by a car. The poor thing was dead, like really, really dead. But, I went back every single day for two weeks to see if, by some chance, it got up and walked home. It never did. But, on the last day I went to see about it, the smell was so overwhelming I vomited on the spot. Multiply that smell by about four hundred and it would come close to this monster's stench. Belatedly, I realized this had been the scent at that warehouse. It had been him.

My throat burned trying to name him. My body hurt not from the pain of the severed connection to Cannon, but of the knowledge of who this man, thing, was. I was shutting down. This was all too much, as he knew it would have been. This place, my friends, this man, it was overwhelming.

"Hello, Addy. I've missed you." His voice was foreign. It sounded pained and gruff.

I didn't answer right away. I grappled, hoping to convince myself that I wasn't seeing this. Praying this wasn't real. *This can't be him.* How had this happened?

A word finally fell from my lips, leaving a burning sensation as though it was pure lava. It was the only word I could have said. His name.

"Aaron."

"Isn't this fun? It's like a family reunion." he hissed.

"How? Why? God, Aaron. Why?" I was in utter shock and disbelief. My childhood hero, my fucking brother. My protector. And now, a monster devoid of everything I once knew.

"I call him the banker." Aaron raised a boney hand to wipe away a drop of green-colored goo that had rolled slowly down his gray chin. "Let's say I owed him a lot of money. So, he offered me this." He gestured to his deteriorating body. "A life of immortality. He'd first offered to change me into a vampire, but that fell through. Then he found this book from a witch."

Fucking Evie. *I am going to ring her goddamned neck the next time I see her pink-clad, Barbie-doll-looking self.*

"It wasn't until after I was changed that I realized he had an ulterior motive. You."

"But, why? Why hurt my friends? Why, Aaron?" I choked the words, desperate to move past the hurt.

"Because I like it. It's fun!" He frowned as if maybe that wasn't really the reason. Maybe it was hopeful thinking that some part of my brother was hidden deep within the monster. He turned, and as he walked deeper into the dark room, I heard a slight squishing noise. It reminded me of the sloshing sound from when there was mud in your shoes. My feet moved without me telling them to do so. I followed, knowing

I was moving, but not sure if it was me or him doing the walking. I heard chains rattling and saw a half-naked Darryl slumped in a heap on the floor. I ran to him. That motion was all me.

"Oh god, god no," I muttered at my hand roamed over him, trying like hell to find a pulse or some kind of life. He was cold and unmoving. *Please, please, please!* My shaking fingers found his throat. I paused to calm my hand. I waited and waited. I felt nothing. I cradled his full face between my hands. His eyes were open, but completely devoid of life.

I looked up at a person I no longer knew, a monster grinning back at me. That was the end of any understanding I might have had for this man.

"Why?" I had no idea why the question slipped out. He couldn't tell me anything that mattered. Not at this point. Darryl was dead.

Aaron peered down, and for the first time, he looked utterly confused. His eyes were pinched with worry, and something I couldn't name sparked behind his once-dead gaze.

"I-I don't know. He-he has my soul. I do as he tells me." His words were ripped from his throat as though he were fighting to get each word out.

"He who?" I asked, getting to my feet. I needed to

get this information. I had to figure out who was be-hind all of this.

"A. Pebble," he rasped. He opened his mouth as if to add more, but nothing other than his black slimy tongue flopped out. He gaped like a fish out of water praying for some kind of relief. I didn't know if I was relieved or pissed off to know that Aaron wasn't A. Pebble.

A deep howl came from behind me, someone I hadn't seen before. Two men held up a thin, emaciated man. I'd looked like that when I hadn't eaten anything other than something that was injected through a vein.

Lifting his head up, his ice-blue eyes pinned me in place. Lachlan. He'd always been a larger man, but now he looked nothing like himself. He wasn't any scruffier, as I didn't think his hair grew in that way, but his face was sunken in and the look he gave me was so feral. He'd been starved.

I saw Theo rounding a tight arc behind Aaron. He still thought this plan was going to work. Boy, was he wrong.

"Aaron why am I here?" I asked, not understanding this.

"I'm going to kill you. I thought that was obvious."

He didn't have to rush me. Clearly our telekinetic ability was something that ran in the family, because I felt my air supply slowly closing as my feet left the floor. And Aaron hadn't moved an inch. Finally, the tears that swam in my eyes spilled warm streaks down my cheeks. Tears for my lost brother, tears for Lachlan, and most of all tears for Darryl.

Black circles danced in my vision. I wanted to give up and just let this happen. Hell, part of me screamed for it. But, FUCK that shit. My eyes popped open and I focused on Aaron, on what used to be my brother. I reached for one of the stones in my left pocket and threw it, hoping against all hope that this worked. I prayed his desperation for his soul took over.

Immediately Aaron's eyes locked on it and that was the only chance I had. His mental grip on my throat lessened and I took that as my chance. I ran as fast as I possibly could. I headed to Lachlan and the men holding him. I didn't care if I killed them. I punched one in the throat then to the side of the head. I was too fast for them to even register anything.

Whirling, I faced the other one, kicking him swiftly in the nuts, and as he fell, I jammed my knee into his jaw. I felt a satisfying crunch of bone. Lachlan stood on his own, but he looked too frail. I quickly noticed that the chains weren't attached to anything other than him. They felt hot. Really fucking hot. I didn't have time to worry about it, so I grabbed him and ran him to the stairs. Our eyes met briefly and I wanted so much to say something to him, anything, but there wasn't time. He was of no use to me with how weak he was, so I left him there, praying he would get out.

I had no idea where Cannon was, so I couldn't waste time. I darted to the farthest corner to see if there was anything I could find before I was literally plucked out of the air and felt iron circle around my right arm. There was a pop followed by agony that spread out in waves along my shoulder and arm. My momentum, along with suddenly stopping, had to have popped my shoulder out of its socket.

Before I could assess the situation, white-hot pain exploded in my chest. *Did I just get shot?* I coughed, trying to inhale, and tasted the metallic tang of blood. I looked down and saw Aaron's fist still balled and pressing against my breast bone. He released me and I staggered backwards. Every time I tried to inhale, a fresh bout of searing pain threatened to overwhelm me. My vision blurred. I'd been hit more times than I could count, but this was nothing like I'd ever felt. Surely if I didn't will my heart to beat, it would stop.

My left hand flew to my chest, as if somehow I could keep the damn thing going.

"A-Aa-Aaron," I croaked. I felt more blood flood my mouth. I tried to spit, but it came out more of a dribble.

"WHERE IS THE SSSSSSSTONE," he hissed. His voice had turned inhuman. It sounded layered, as if there were twenty voices speaking at once. Though, that could have all been in my head for all I knew.

I fell to my knees, managing to grab the last stone in my left pocket. I could only manage to toss it a few feet before I slumped farther to the ground.

"Addison!" I heard a voice call. It might have been Theo's, but I wasn't sure.

"Theo, get Lachlan out of here!" Now that voice I knew. It was Cannon. But, everything was blurring.

Aaron let out a deafening cry. I thought the sheer volume of it would topple the already unsteady house. I tried to cover my ears, but my right arm hung lifeless and unmoving. I had to get to the real stone in my right pocket.

I reached with my left hand. Just as my fingers brushed the cool jagged stone, I saw Aaron rush me. Closing my eyes, I braced myself for his impact, only it never came. I opened my eyes to see a bloody Cannon and Lachlan raining blows down on Aaron.

My eyes narrowed, not understanding how in hell Lachlan was even on his feet much less able to move like that. Theo lay slumped against an opposing wall. His eyes were open and a small smile spread across his face. He gave me a weak thumb's up. I returned my attention to the three men. Aaron looked as though the two men were nothing more than an annoyance.

I saw movement out of the corner of my eye. Shit, the two men that held Lachlan were waking up. I was out of time.

Can I do this? Can I be the one to end my brother's life? My gaze fell on Darryl's lifeless body. The only father I'd ever had. The only one who loved me and didn't want something from me. Whoever this monster was, he was no longer my brother. Aaron had died long ago. He'd died in a quest to save me. He'd died keeping his promise to save me. Now, it was my turn to save him.

I felt the heated stone in my hand. Confused, I looked down, grasping it. *How did it get there?* I looked up and was met with Aaron's dead blue eyes. I didn't have the physical strength to do this. So, I would have to rely on my mental abilities.

Aaron lurched forward. I only had a moment. I slammed my hand down to the ground and at the same time I pushed hard mentally, creating an unstoppable force. My hand slammed so hard into the ground I felt the delicate bones break. None of the pain mattered. Aaron's eyes flashed bright with life.

In that moment, my brother was back, the shell that was his body overflowing with light and warmth. He fell to his knees only inches from me. His blue eyes sparkled with life and what looked to be black tears. I wanted to say something, do anything. Words failed me. All I could do was watch him catch his breath one pained gasp at a time. This creature was my brother, his soul had returned and my heart seemed to know he'd come back. I had visions of him brushing my pale hair while our mother was passed out on the couch or had some guy in her room. He'd taken care of me and I'll never forget that. I tried to smile at him, to let him know I knew who he was. I knew he was once again the child I'd remembered, but the pain was excruciating. His gnarled jaw began moving as though he were trying to speak.

"Thank you for freeing me. I'm sorry I couldn't do the same for you." With that, a black tar type of liquid oozed out of his mouth, nostrils, and eyes just before he fell backwards. The scent of death assailed me. I tried to retch, but my chest hurt so bad that I nearly blacked out from the involuntary action.

My chest felt heavy and my breathing was becoming labored. I felt like I was drowning. My deep gasps for air turned into short, shallow intakes. I raised my mangled hand to my chest, willing myself to heal. I couldn't die. I slumped to the floor. Wait, no, I was helped to the floor. Someone was behind me, guiding me.

"Addison, can you hear me?" It was Lachlan's frantic tone. I tried to nod but I wasn't too sure I was able to get the motion out.

"Stop. I can't heal you. I'm too weak and damnit, Addison, it's too much! My blood would do no good!" His Scottish accent was so pronounced I wanted to giggle.

My left hand still laid over my chest. I closed my eyes. I pulled all of my power, all of my speed, telekinetic ability, and pure will, and focused it. My own hand felt hot, but oh so welcomed. After a few moments, I was able to breathe a deep, much-needed breath. I gasped once more and sank into Lachlan's arms.

"Simply amazing," I heard a distant voice. I had no idea if it was someone speaking to me or in my head. My eyes tried to flicker open, but all of my will to stay awake fled and I sank further into a welcoming darkness.

Chapter Twenty-Two

When I next opened my eyes, I was met with bright, white lights. I shut them tightly and groaned.

"Turn off the goddamned lights," I croaked. Was that my voice? I sounded like I'd smoked twenty-seven packs a day for thirteen years. Yuck.

"Stop being a pussy," a female voice snapped.

Groaning again, I managed to say, "Gen. Water." I still refused to open my eyes.

"Here."

I felt the poke of a straw at my lips. I drank deeply. While the cold liquid was refreshing, it burned going down.

"Slow down. You're going to choke and die and then I'll be blamed for it," she chided as she pulled the straw from my lips.

"Thanks. Douche monster," I rasped.

She nearly choked.

"Okay. Fine, the lights are off."

I peeked under one eyelid to see if she was being an ass. The lights were indeed off but hell, it was still bright. I decided to just rip the Band-Aid off and open them. I was only blinded for a moment before the shapes and colors of the dim room sharpened into focus. I had a thousand questions, but only one singular pressing need.

"Gen, can you help me over to the bathroom?" I hated to ask her anything, much less this, but I was left with few options.

Eyeing me dubiously, she muttered, "Fine, but I'm not wiping for you."

"Go fall on a stake," I groaned as she helped me to my feet.

About ten minutes later, I emerged on my own. No need for assistance for this pusher.

I knew I was at Cannon's but not in his room, thankfully. I still felt a little off about what happened between us and did not need to add anything to that. Thankfully, though, there was a toothbrush and toothpaste and I took full advantage. I couldn't look at myself in the mirror. I just couldn't face myself yet.

Lachlan, Cannon, and Gen were all standing in the small room. *Now that I think of it, this is the room Theo had been in.*

All three of them looked utterly pissed off with me. Wonderful. *I wake up and everyone is mad as fuck at me. I should have stayed asleep.*

I walked over to the bed and sat down.

"What the fuck is wrong with all of you?"

At my question Gen left the room muttering, "I want no part of this."

My eyes fell on Lachlan. He still looked thin, but not near as gaunt. His pale-blue eyes sparked with displeasure, but sparkled nonetheless. Just seeing him filled me with warmth that I couldn't explain.

Then they explained what they knew.

Aaron had taken Lachlan. He'd had a whole lot of help from the turned pushers. Apparently when Theo and I went to that warehouse, we'd been so close to Lachlan and Aaron that all we needed to do was walk in. That information about killed me, because it could have saved Darryl.

I asked Cannon why he severed our connection. His explanation was that he tried to keep Aaron from using him against me. He'd feared his pusher ability, even though we hadn't known what they were. It was all preemptive. So nice of him to inform me that he was going to sever my brain in two with a freaking lightsaber. Cannon's men had been able to take out some of the turned pushers, but not all. Once Cannon showed up, they scattered like cockroaches.

"Why couldn't you have told me? I thought you were dead!" My question came out a little more serious than I meant it, but damn.

"He was more than a telekinetic. He had the ability to control someone's body. That's likely why whoever changed him picked him. You know how rare it is for a pusher to have two abilities," Cannon explained in a belittling tone. I rolled my eyes, all the while wondering if there was a little of my old Aaron in there. He could have used that ability against me but didn't. I guess I'll never truly know.

"What about the money man? I gathered that Aaron wasn't A. Pebble," I asked, scooting back on the bed. My feet were left dangling, making me feel more like a child, but I really didn't care. My whole body hurt.

"Still nothing. Brent's working on a money trail from your brother's accounts, but there's nothing there. And it looks like A. Pebble is still out there," Lachlan explained. I flinched at the mention of the word *brother*. I couldn't help it. That monster wasn't my brother.

"This feels like we are running in circles chasing our own tails. Always one step behind."

I glanced down and noticed my hand wasn't in a splint or cast. I raised it up to eye level and inspected it. I wiggled my fingers and expected there to be pain, but there was none.

"Lachlan, did you?"

He shook his head.

"Well then how-"

"You did it," Theo's voice sounded from the doorway. I looked up to see his bright face peering down at me. I nearly launched myself off the mattress and rounded the corner of the bed, flying into his outstretched arms. He was my person. He was family of my heart.

His big arms tightened around me and I felt the soft press of his lips on the top of my head. I pushed all thoughts about healing aside.

His big brown eyes met mine. He was so warm. He was everything I ever wanted in a brother.

"Are you okay?" I whispered, setting my chin on his chest.

"Always, chickadee." He gave me one more squeeze and led me back to the edge of the bed.

"If it weren't for Theo, I wouldn't have been able to do a damn thing." Lachlan's tone held a note of appreciation.

"Hey, buddy, no worries. I'm sure it tasted good going down."

I raised an eyebrow to Lachlan and saw his blue eyes flicker to ice before he looked away.

"Um, could y'all leave so I could speak with Lachlan for a few?"

Theo nodded and left. Cannon, however, didn't budge. *Please don't make me bitch slap your pointy toothed ass,* I didn't say.

Lachlan's gaze was focused firmly in the other direction than myself. I sighed.

"Cannon," I started but was silenced by his hand.

Pushing himself off the wall, he said, "Make a choice, Addison." He left the room with not even a glance back.

I had four hundred things I wanted to say to Lachlan, but I couldn't seem to formulate a single word, much less a string of them to form a thought.

Without a word, he got up. I was struck suddenly with how utterly attractive he was. His frame was still thinner than I was used to, but his piercing blue eyes were no longer sunken in. Feeding was doing his body right.

"Lachlan I need-"

"Addison let me make-"

We both started at the same time. I laughed and gestured with my hand for him to continue.

I was desperately trying to read him. His face gave nothing other than complete detachment. I bit my lower lip and played with the edge of the sheet that had bunched just under my right thigh.

"Addison, I'm thankful you found me. There's nothing I could do to thank you for everything." He still refused to meet my eyes. I knew the other shoe was about to drop. "Addison, let me make your choice easy. I'm out. Just like you once told me, I'm done with you."

He turned, his shoulders bunching with tension. He paused with his hand on the doorknob. *Look back, Lachlan. Please!* my mind was screaming.

He walked out of the room and didn't glance back at all.

I waited for an innumerable amount of minutes, staring at the door. It was painted white. I could see the wood grain running along its smooth surface.

Finally, I found my voice. I said the words I'd wanted to say to him for some time.

"I'm sorry. I was wrong. I know why you did what you did. I should have never cut you off. I was so wrong." I closed my eyes. I wished like hell this was a dream. Unfortunately, this was the bed that I made.

Now, I had to pull up my own big girl panties and lay in it.

Willing my body to sleep, I couldn't seem to push Lachlan's words out of my mind.

"I'm done with you."

"I'm done with me, too."

Epilogue

THREE WEEKS LATER

Darryl's funeral had been two weeks ago but I still felt helpless and broken over his loss. I laid down on my bed, staring up at the ceiling fan making a slow spinning circle. I felt like a fan, slowly spinning, never really going anywhere. Making the same mistakes, never really getting anything right. I was having a pity party and I knew it. I was pathetic and I didn't really care.

I'd ignored everyone. Theo had been calling, hell even Gen had tried. I was simply one fracture away from breaking. Though if I were to admit it, as an addict, I was always a moment away.

I stood up and walked over to the mirror on my closet door. The person looking back at me was unknown. And, really fucking pathetic. I was so done feeling sorry for myself. I ran into the bathroom, tossed on my running clothes, and threw my hair up in a bun. I needed to find me again. I needed to scrape myself off the sidewalk and get my shit straight.

Grabbing my keys, I walked to the front door. I swung it open and was met by a short stocky man.

"Uh," was all the man could say.

"Uh, hi, can I help you?" We were about the same height, so we were able to fully look one another in the eye. A really strange experience, as I wasn't used to it.

"Are you Addison…" He paused and looked down at a file he held in his hand.

"Fitzpatrick?" I answered for him.

His rather large head bobbed in affirmation.

"Here this is for you," he said, handing me the file.

Turning to walk away he added, "If you have questions regarding the inheritance, please contact the number on the card." Without another word he disappeared down the stairs.

"Inheritance?" I asked no one. I turned and walked back into my apartment.

I opened the file and began reading.

"Goddamn you, Darryl," I sighed.

He'd left me the fucking dojo. Tears rolled down my cheeks and there was little I could do to stop them. He'd written me a letter explaining why, but I just couldn't make myself read past the first few lines. I tossed the papers down and bolted out the door, down the stairs, and out into the cold February day. I was gasping for air. I needed more and couldn't seem to take enough in. I did the only thing I was ever good at. I ran.

The world melted away. All I was left with was my slamming heartbeat. I pushed everything back and away, letting the cold February air sing to my exposed skin. I welcomed every moment of the biting pain.

Everything I wanted this run to be, cathartic and freeing, it wasn't. It was fleeing and avoiding. I had no direction, no idea where I would end up, but I found in that moment I didn't care. I let my feet take me.

The bright blues and yellows of daytime melted into the dark burnt oranges of early evening. I only noticed because the blurred scenery started to darken. I stopped. I could have been in a hundred places two states away.

My vision began to clear and the building I stood in front of came into focus. I wanted to laugh. I wanted to find something funny about where my body wanted to take me. But, I couldn't.

This was the rundown apartment of one of my drug dealers. This, however, wasn't just any drug dealer. We had a history of sorts.

I wanted to leave. I willed my body to run back to my apartment. My feet moved, but closer to the building.

It had been years. He was likely dead or moved at the very least.

Why couldn't I stop myself? I reached out and pressed the button that had been Marcus's apartment.

I turned away, finally.

"Hello, who's there?" a heavy male, tinny voice sounded from the intercom.

I whirled and pressed the button and couldn't stop the words coming from my mouth.

"It's Addison. Marcus?" *God, why did I say that?*

"Yeah, but who..." He paused. I tried like hell to run. I tried to turn my ass around but I couldn't make myself budge. *What is wrong with me?*

"Oh, yeah. Blonde chick from back in the day. It's been a while, but I got your shit. I got you, no worries. Come on up. Let's call it a Valentine's Day special. That's today right?"

I nodded. Not that he could see.

The door buzzed open. I reached to the latch and pulled it slightly. *What the fuck are you doing?* My brain was screaming to stop. This was more than playing with fire. But, all I could seem to recall was my first high. All I could seem to remember was the burn, the euphoria of all of my problems being lifted gingerly away...

I pulled the door open and walked through.

TO BE CONTINUED IN

BOOK THREE OF THE VAMPIRE FAVORS SERIES

Fight or Flight

Playlist

Slip – Elliot Moss
Congratulations – Rachel Platten
Beating Me Up - Rachel Platten
Lone Ranger- Rachel Platten
Fight Song - Rachel Platten
Angle of Small Death and the Codeine Scene – Hozier
Work Song – Hozier
Foreigner's God – Hozier
Roots – Imagine Dragons
Stay – Rihanna
Burning House – Cam
Same Old Love – Selena Gomez
Blurryface – Twenty-one Piolets
Make it Rain – Ed Sheeran
Up in Flames – Ruelle
Until We Go Down – Ruelle

About the Author

Emily Cyr is a stay-at-home mom turned writer. She holds a degree in middle grades education with certification in English and social science. She has always had a love of all things paranormal and fantasy, but it wasn't until Emily's husband said the words, "Why not?" that she considered putting her thoughts and ideas into the book, The Lightning Prophecy. This trilogy was just the start for Emily. It seemed to open a creative door that had been locked.

Emily has always been an avid reader. Through reading came her love of writing. The more she read, the more she knew she wanted to create her own world. Many of her first works were fan fiction.

Emily and her family currently reside in Jacksonville, Florida. She has an incredibly supportive husband. They have two sons, ages 5, 4, and 3 months. Somehow, even with the demands of being a parent to three little boys, she finds time to escape to her fantasies and write them down.

Currently, Emily has two urban fantasy series out, but stay tuned via her web-site, www.EmilyCyr.com, for more!

Did you enjoy this book? Please leave a quick review on Amazon! Nine out of ten authors agree, reviews make them happy. The tenth author was shot for not agreeing. Don't worry, he lived, but he learned his lesson.

Made in the USA
Columbia, SC
06 September 2017